Cloud Juice

Cloud Juice

Believe in yourself
and anything is possible.
LaRue

By LaRue Roth

Unlimited Publishing
Bloomington, Indiana

Distributing Publisher:
Unlimited Publishing LLC
Bloomington, Indiana

http://www.unlimitedpublishing.com

Contributing Publisher:
LaRue Roth

Cover and book design by Charles King. Copyright © 2004 by Unlimited Publishing LLC. This book was typeset with Adobe® InDesign®, using the Adobe Garamond® typeface. This book makes use of one or more typefaces specifically licensed by and customized for the exclusive use of Unlimited Publishing LLC.

First edition.

Copies of this fine book and others
are available to order online at:

http://www.unlimitedpublishing.com/authors

ISBN 1-58832-112-6

Unlimited Publishing
Bloomington, Indiana

Dedicated to

God, the source of all creation,

My beloved daughter, Megan, who is the light of my life,

and

The little towheaded boy who lived on Barbe Street.

Chapter 1

"Look – there in the sky. A fire-breathing dragon is heading toward the castle," cried out the tall, blond-haired boy, his blue eyes gazing upward. He crossed his ankles, putting one high-topped sneaker over the other, and turned to stare into the intense brown eyes of his fellow knight. "We're doomed."

"Never. First, we must warn the king. Then we'll fight the horrible dragon, save the villagers and rescue the beautiful princess Allison," replied his brave friend-in-arms who waved his grape popsicle at the dragon now soaring overhead.

A woman's voice called out from a window high above them. Unfortunately, it was not the beautiful princess who spoke. "Elliot Jonathan Brown you better have that fence painted by the time your father gets home."

"Oh, mom. We're just taking a break," Elliot hollered back at her. He and Miguel were lying on the carpet of grass in the Brown front yard, watching large, puffy clouds sail in and out of view. A parade of monsters and wild beasts passed over them as the clouds shifted and swirled.

He rolled over onto his stomach and glanced up at his mother who was leaning out of an upstairs window of their house. Elliot's mother never called him by his full name unless she was really steamed at him. She gave him a weak smile and ducked back into the house.

"If you wouldn't have ruined your dad's new camera, you wouldn't be stuck here working," Miguel said with a sigh, wishing he and Elliot were down by the river skipping rocks on this warm, muggy Saturday afternoon in early May.

"I didn't mean to break it. How was I supposed to know the dumb camera didn't work under water?" Elliot asked in a puzzled voice. "Maybe it'll rain," he added hopefully, looking back up at the fluffy clouds overhead as he sat up and grabbed a brush.

"Hurry up and finish so we can go to the river. I bet the fish are biting," Miguel said impatiently.

"If you would help me, we could be out of here in 20 minutes," Elliot said as he whacked the picket fence hard with the paintbrush, sending specks of white paint flying in every direction. Elliot hated to paint and this was the fourth Saturday afternoon in a row he had spent working on the picket fence that ran along the front of the house.

"I'm entertaining you. That's helping." Miguel sank into the hammock with a smug look on his tan face.

They grew quiet while Elliot slapped paint onto the wood as fast as he could. Miguel closed his eyes lost in one of his favorite daydreams, the one where he starred in his own television series. A small airplane droned overhead and then faded into the distance. Crocket, Elliot's yellow Labrador dog, napped under a huge, live oak tree shading the yard. The dog sat up, yawned and flopped back down on the grass.

Then without warning there was a huge SPLAT. Something cold and wet exploded on Elliot's head. Icy, cold liquid ran down his neck and shoulders.

"Hey, knock it off," Elliot yelled as he whirled around in time to see a green blob splatter on Miguel's face. SPLAT. SPLAT. The bombs were falling faster now. Elliot took another direct hit from above him and let out a squeal.

"We're under attack," Miguel screamed as he tumbled onto the ground.

"Head for cover," Elliot yelled as both boys dived under the picnic table.

Sharp laughter rang out from among the branches in the oak tree above the boys. They peeked out from under the table just as a skinny, wild-eyed girl with a tangle of long, brown hair dropped from a lower limb of the tree and shouted, "Gotcha."

"Get her, Crocket," Elliot commanded as the boys quickly scrambled out from under the picnic table and ran toward their attacker.

"Tackle her to the ground," chimed in Miguel.

Crocket charged over to the girl who immediately knelt down and threw her arms around the dog's neck. She closed her eyes and let Crocket lick every inch of her face.

"Hey, you got my hair wet," Miguel complained as he ran a hand through the thick, black mop on his head.

"Stop whining, you big baby," Hannah said, a wide grin lighting up her face. "It looked like you two needed some excitement." She turned her attention back to Crocket whose tail was wagging furiously. The dog clearly adored Hannah and for good reason.

Elliot and his parents had moved to Cypress Springs just before school started last August. As workers unloaded their furniture from the moving van the day they arrived, Elliot had noticed a scrawny girl riding her bike back and forth on the street in front of their new home. It was Hannah, although he hadn't known her name then.

She wore a baseball cap backward over her pigtails, showing off a puffy, black eye on the right side of her face. Since she was a girl, he pretended not to notice her and eventually she rode away. Within a few days he became best friends with Miguel, who lived a few doors down the block.

A couple months later though, Crocket befriended Hannah – girl or no girl. It happened one day as Elliot and Miguel were on their way home from the convenience store. As they turned the corner of the block onto their street, they saw two older boys chasing a dog down the middle of the road. One of the redheaded bullies was trying to pull the dog's tail; the other was swinging a big stick at the pooch.

Elliot turned pale and dropped the half-gallon of milk he was carrying. "Crocket, come here boy," he yelled as he took off running down the street toward his dog. Miguel was right beside him as they raced as fast as they could.

Before Elliot and Miguel could reach Crocket, they saw a pint-sized tornado collide with the two bullies. "Why don't you pick on someone your own size, you big meanies," Hannah screamed at the McGruder brothers who were almost twice as big as she was. The girl pelted them with rocks and kicked one of the boys in the shin hard.

The older boys were momentarily stunned. The girl took advantage of their confusion and grabbed Crocket's collar. "C'mon . . . we've gotta run," she cried out, urging the dog on. Hannah and the dog reached the Brown house just as Miguel and Elliot came running up.

They all stood there looking at each other for a few minutes, too out of breath to even speak. Elliot knelt down and ran his fingers through his dog's fur coat, checking to see if he had been hurt. "Thanks for saving Crocket," Elliot finally said solemnly, looking up at Hannah. "Wanna come in and eat chocolate chip cookies with us?" Hannah smiled broadly and nodded.

"Earth to Elliot," Miguel shouted in his ear, bringing Elliot back to the present. "What are you going to compete in at Field Day? It's next Friday."

Elliot groaned and sprawled back down on the grass. "I guess whatever event I get stuck with," he said. Since he was tall for his age, Elliot was expected to excel at sports, but he really didn't enjoy competition. Elliot's dad said he lacked confidence and coordination.

"I wish I'd win at something, though. Then my parents could think up a way to reward me for a change." Elliot saw the summer ahead filled with an endless list of chores. His parents called them "consequences for his actions." He groaned again.

"Hey y'all want to go have some fun?" Hannah asked, changing the subject. She waved a half-filled bag of empty water bomb balloons in their faces. "Your sisters are sunbathing in your backyard, Miguel."

"Can't. Gotta paint," Elliot spat out.

"See you *mañana*," Miguel shouted over his shoulder as he took off after Hannah. He couldn't resist the chance to torment his sisters. Elliot watched his friends dash out of the yard and down the street.

"No fair," muttered Elliot, picking up the paintbrush. Just as he started to paint the last slat, Elliot's nose informed him somebody in the neighborhood was grilling hamburgers. His stomach told him to hurry up and finish his work.

"That's a mighty fine job you're doing there, young man." Elliot glanced up to see a tall, brown-haired man standing on the sidewalk on the other side of the fence. The stranger looked hot and uncomfortable wearing a dark business suit and tie. Sweat trickled down the side of his face.

Elliot was flattered by the man's praise, but uncomfortable about talking to someone he didn't know. "I guess," he muttered, his face flushed red with embarrassment. He had been warned many times not to talk to strangers.

"I'm looking for the home of Professor Edward T. Brown. I understand he lives here on Austin Street," the stranger said.

"That's my grandpa. He lives over there," Elliot replied in surprise, pointing to the house next door. He figured the man must be someone from the college where his grandfather taught part time, but Elliot didn't remember seeing him before.

Elliot heard his name shouted from the direction he had pointed. "Hey, that's my grandpa calling me now. I'll go tell him you're here to see him," Elliot offered and took off running across the yard.

He opened the vine-covered gate separating the two yards and followed his nose to the sizzling hamburgers. "Hi, grandpa. That smells soooo good."

His grandfather, wearing an apron over his big tummy, turned and gave Elliot a broad smile. "Thought you might like a burger and a milkshake after working so hard all afternoon," he said. "Are you almost done painting so we can eat?" A picnic table, covered with a red-checkered tablecloth, was set with four place settings. That meant he and his parents would be joining his grandfather for dinner.

"Just about." Elliot poured a tall glass of iced tea from a pitcher setting on the picnic table. He gulped it down and wiped his mouth with the back of his hand. "Oh . . . There's a man waiting outside our fence who wants to talk to you," Elliot said. He had almost forgotten about the stranger when he saw the feast waiting on the picnic table.

Spatula in hand, Professor Brown followed Elliot back through the gate and across the front yard to meet the stranger. There was no one standing by the fence.

"Elliot are you sure there was someone looking for me?" his grandfather quizzed, his bushy, dark gray eyebrows raised. Elliot ran out to the sidewalk and looked up and down the street in confusion. The only person he saw was Mrs. Klepp pushing a baby stroller down the sidewalk.

"Honest, grandpa. There was a man wearing a suit who asked where you lived," Elliot said, feeling foolish. "He knew your name."

Professor Brown laughed and put his arm around Elliot's shoulder, "Son, someday that imagination of yours is either going to make you rich or get you into a lot of trouble."

Chapter 2

"What time are you leaving for the airport?" Elliot heard his mom call up the stairs to his father early Monday morning. "Have you seen my green polo shirt?" a male voice drifted back down to her.

Elliot sat at the kitchen table staring at the back of a breakfast cereal box in a daze. "Yuck," he frowned. "Today I'll have to try out for Field Day events in P.E. class."

"Hurry up and eat. You'll be late for school," his mother whispered to him before sticking the telephone back to her ear. "Jon will be out of town on business until Friday afternoon. What about Saturday?" she went on speaking into the telephone.

Jon Brown hurried into the kitchen with a travel bag in both hands and leaned over to kiss Elliot's mom smack on the lips. "Double yuck," muttered Elliot as he watched them. His dad set both bags down on the floor and slid his tall frame into a chair next to Elliot, staring intently at his son through his wire-framed glasses.

"I'm counting on you to take care of your mom while I'm gone this week," he said affectionately. "And please stay out of trouble," he added hopefully. "See this," he said, pointing to the gray hair sprouting among his light brown hair and neatly groomed beard. "I get another gray hair every time you have one of your wild adventures." He grinned at Elliot and Elliot smiled back but only one side of his mouth went up. Elliot sighed. He didn't mean to give his dad gray hair.

"I'll call you and your mom tonight when I get to Seattle." Elliot's father grabbed his luggage and headed out the back door to his car, which was parked in the garage behind the house.

The weather continued to be hot and steamy; students and teachers at the Cypress Springs Elementary School were restless in their classrooms. The fourth and fifth grade students exploded onto the playground in mid afternoon for P.E. class, happy to be outside.

"All you boys come stand around me over here," Coach Meadows bellowed. Elliot and Miguel trailed behind the pack as their classmates jostled and pushed their way over to the coach.

"You all know Field Day is coming up on Friday," the coach continued. "I've assigned most of you to one or more events. Today we're going to work on the long jump and the relay race. I'll be watching to see who can float through the air," said Coach Meadows, laughing at her own bad joke.

Elliot was told to file off with the group heading toward the long jump pit and Miguel was sent with the group starting relay races. After awhile the groups switched places. The final school bell rang and everyone scattered.

"I can't believe it," Elliot griped as he, Miguel and Hannah walked home from school. "All you have to do for Field Day is videotape it?" He glared at Miguel.

"Coach Meadows thought it was a cool idea," Miguel said proudly, flashing his movie star smile.

Hannah laughed and Elliot turned to her. "I suppose you'll be in every girls' race," he said with envy. No one could outrun Hannah.

"A couple of 'em. How about you?" she replied.

Elliot kicked at a rock on the sidewalk. "I tripped and fell during the relay race and stepped over the board when I was doing the long jump," he said glumly.

Miguel spotted the El Toro River that flowed through the middle of Cypress Springs just ahead. Hoping to make Elliot forget about his bad luck, he said, "Let's take the long way home and go hang out at the river for awhile." A city park ran along one side of the river for about half a mile and it included a long, narrow island in the middle of the river as well.

They hurried across the low water crossing of the river and headed for the city park. "Race ya," Hannah called out, speeding ahead of the two boys across the concrete walking bridge that ran between the riverbank and the island. Not even the heavy backpack she carried slowed her down enough for the two boys to catch up to her.

Along with fire ants and armadillos, low water crossing signs had been a mystery to Elliot when he first moved to the Texas hill country. Miguel had explained that the tall, narrow signs, numbered from bottom to top, warned drivers how much water was covering the road if a river was overflowing. Even a couple feet of water washing over a highway could sweep a car and its passengers into flooded creeks or rivers.

Usually a gentle stream, the El Toro River could become like a raging bull when large amounts of rain fell in a short time. But today the El Toro was calm. Majestic bald cypress trees lined the banks of the river and dotted the island. A green heron stood motionless in the middle of the shallow channel of the river, waiting for its dinner to swim by.

A clump of three cypress trees at the far end of the island was a favorite hideaway for Hannah, Miguel and Elliot. They spent hours there telling each other secrets and acting out stories Miguel made up for them.

Hannah was already scampering up one of the trees that leaned gently over the bank when the boys arrived. From there she grabbed a limb of the taller middle tree and started to climb. "I'm gonna see if our stuff is still hidden in the hollow."

Miguel and Elliot followed Hannah up the tree and squeezed past her when she stopped to stick her arm into a small, hollowed out spot in the Cypress tree. The boys inched out onto a limb midway up the tree to make room for them all to sit. For a little while, they rested quietly and watched the river flow by.

Then Elliot yanked off his shoes and socks, letting them drop to the riverbank below.

"No way . . . you're *loco*," Miguel sputtered. "The water's not warm enough yet."

Hannah yelped in glee. "I dare you. I double dare you. I triple dare you."

Without a word, Elliot reached across Hannah and grabbed the end of a long rope that was hooked to the tree. Clinging to the rope, he jumped from the limb. As Elliot swung over the middle of the deep, river channel, he let go of the rope.

There was a loud splash. Elliot screeched as his head broke the surface of the water a few seconds later and he swam for shore. "COLD. Really, really cold."

Hannah and Miguel climbed down in time to watch Elliot drag himself up onto the bank, looking like a bedraggled river rat dressed in walking shorts and a T-shirt. A big grin spread across Elliot's face as he shook himself like a dog, spraying his friends with water. It was the first time he had smiled all day.

Chapter 3

"Mom, I'm home," Elliot called out as the threesome stampeded into the Brown house and headed for the kitchen. Since Elliot's mother worked on a computer from her home office, she encouraged Elliot to invite his friends home after school.

Chattering voices and laughter filled the kitchen. "Need some help in there?" his mother called out, hearing the refrigerator door open and close and cupboard doors slam.

Elliot glanced down at his muddy, wet clothes. It would be better if he dried off before his mother saw him. "We're gonna go see what grandpa's doing," he replied as he carefully set their milk glasses in the kitchen sink. They each grabbed a handful of oatmeal cookies and headed for the back door.

"You're lucky to have such a cool grandpa," said Hannah, feeding one of her cookies to Crocket as they walked across the grass.

"Not only is he cool, he's famous," continued Miguel eagerly.

Elliot didn't think of his grandfather as cool or famous. Since his dad was often gone on business, Elliot enjoyed spending time with his grandfather, tinkering around the professor's sunny workshop in his backyard. That's usually where Elliot could find him this time of day.

Trying to squeeze through the workshop door all at once, Elliot and his friends could hear a woman's voice mingling with the professor's. They hurried past rows of tables filled with potted plants, beakers and racks of test tubes, curious to see who the visitor was. Gadgets and instruments of different sizes were scattered all around the room on shelves, most of them in pieces.

"Here comes the pack." Professor Brown's blue eyes sparkled when he saw his newest guests. He reached over and tousled Elliot and Miguel's hair and winked at Hannah. "What happened to you, Elliot? Fall in the river?" he joked.

"Ya, sorta," Elliot stammered, suddenly shy as he glanced at the woman standing next to his grandfather. She was very pretty. The lime green pantsuit she wore set off her short, curly, copper-colored hair. Toenails polished blood red peeked out from the front of her high-heeled sandals.

Professor Brown said, "This is Mrs. Paula Ripkin. She's interviewing me for a story she is doing."

"Are you from Hollywood?" Miguel asked in awe. His question made the woman laugh, a high grating noise.

"Oh no. I write for a health magazine and Professor Brown was just telling me about the fascinating research he's done in the field of weather modification," she said, beaming a huge smile at the professor.

"What's weather modification?" asked Hannah, stumbling over the last word. She hung back, suspicious of the highly perfumed woman who held everyone's attention.

"That's when people try to change the weather," Professor Brown said. "For example, cloud seeding programs are being used to try to help it rain more in dry places like West Texas. Some people believe that cloud seeding also might be useful in preventing hailstorms so farm crops aren't damaged."

"Do they use bird seed or plant seed? And how do you get it to stay in the clouds? Wouldn't it just fall right through?" Hannah demanded, firing off one question right after the other. She imagined people lighting up the sky with cloud seeding rockets like the Fourth of July only to have it rain birdseed back down on their heads.

The red-haired lady laughed too loud. "Kids say the cutest things," she said with a smirk, fluttering her eyes at Professor Brown. Hannah glared at the woman

Professor Brown smiled at Hannah encouragingly. "Those are great questions, Hannah. Cloud seeding does sound like an impossible idea. Actually, pilots and scientists fly airplanes into promising rain clouds and release a small amount of a special chemical that causes raindrops to form."

Elliot had listened to his grandfather talk about his work many times. He chimed in, hoping to impress the writer. "Even the military is working on ways to control the weather to help them win wars. Right grandpa?" His grandfather nodded and smiled.

"Tell me about the newest invention you're working on, professor," the red-haired woman said in her bubbly voice. "I've heard rumors about some kind of power drink you are developing from rain water. Will it really make people smarter and perform better at sports?" she rattled on. "May I see your machine? What are you going to call it?

Professor Brown was clearly overjoyed by her attention and for the chance to talk about his work. "Let me show you my Cloud Juicer. Of course there is still much work to be done on it. I'm just about to begin testing it on plants," he added modestly.

Elliot, Miguel and Hannah crowded around to look at the Cloud Juicer too. "You kids run along now so Mrs. Ripkin and I can talk. I'll show it to you later," said the professor kindly, nudging Elliot toward the door.

They plopped down on the grass outside the workshop and munched on the rest of their cookies. Elliot chose a sunny spot to sit, hoping his clothes would dry quickly. Crocket lay down beside him, intently sniffing the delicious river smells on his T-shirt.

"I don't like that woman," Hannah pronounced, wrinkling her nose. "She must've dumped a whole bottle of perfume on her head."

"What's not to like?" Miguel said with a big grin. "You're jealous because she's so beautiful."

"You think she's beautiful? I bet it takes two hours every night to scrub all that makeup off her face. And she could poke someone's eye out with those long, fingernails."

Elliot barely listened to them argue back and forth. He sat very still as a red wasp slowly circled around his head. In a couple minutes the wasp sped off like a tiny helicopter on a mission. He was thinking about his grandfather, how everyone seemed to like him and admire him.

"Ah ha!" shouted Elliot. "I know how I can win an event at Field Day."

Miguel and Hannah stopped bickering and stared at him in alarm. They'd seen that faraway look in Elliot's eyes before – just before the three of them got into trouble. Big trouble.

"I don't like it when you get your big ideas." Miguel plucked at the grass while looking at Elliot nervously.

"Spit it out Einstein," Hannah commanded. She wanted to hear Elliot's plan for winning an event at Field Day.

"The Cloud Juice," Elliot said in a hushed voice.

"What about the Cloud Juice?" Miguel asked.

"Remember what that lady said? Cloud Juice makes people smarter and better at sports. If I drink Cloud Juice, I'll win the long jump and mom and dad and grandpa will think I'm really wonderful," Elliot rattled on, jumping up in excitement and waving his arms around. "Then for sure we'll take that vacation to Yellowstone National Park this summer I've heard them talking about." Crocket started to bark as if he were agreeing.

"Awesome," Miguel spoke up. He thought that Elliot's idea was brilliant. He was also relieved that the plan didn't include anything that would get *him* into trouble.

"Have you completely lost your mind Elliot Brown?" Hannah asked sharply. She jumped up from where she sat and stood directly in front of Elliot with her hands on her hips. Her face was flushed in anger.

Elliot didn't like the way Hannah was acting. She was sounding an awful lot like his mother. "What's your problem?" he demanded, crossing his arms over his chest.

"You're gonna take drugs? That's your big idea?" she asked in an accusing voice.

"Not drugs, dummy," he grumped back. "Cloud Juice isn't a drug. It's something my grandpa invented."

"It's something he's going to experiment with on plants, not on people you . . . you . . . bird brain," Hannah shouted back. "You want to end up like my brother Brian?" her voice rising to a squeak. Brian, who was 16, had swallowed a couple pills a friend handed him at a party without even asking what they were. He'd almost died because of it.

Elliot blinked rapidly; his heart pounded in anger. He and Hannah stood glaring at each other. Neither of them would give an inch of ground.

"It's not dope!" Elliot waved his arms wildly in frustration.

"No, you're the dope!" Hannah jabbed Elliot in the chest with her finger.

Miguel watched his friends unhappily, trying to think of some way to end the fight. "Maybe she's right, Elliot," he said in a soothing voice. "Ask your grandpa if the Cloud Juice is okay for people to drink."

But it was too late. Elliot wasn't about to back down now. "You're just a big sissy," he hissed at Hannah.

Elliot regretted the words as soon they left his mouth. Nothing made Hannah madder than being called a sissy. Elliot had seen the revenge she handed out to her brothers more than once for teasing her about being a girl. It was usually painful.

He and Miguel got mad at each sometimes, but their spats usually lasted for two minutes. They'd slug each other or yell and then forget about it. Not Hannah. Hannah would hold a grudge for days. Sometimes she'd get over it and act like nothing happened. Sometimes when you least expected it, she would strike back.

"I hope you turn green and your toes shrivel up and fall off," she replied icily. Hannah grabbed her schoolbag and stomped away, leaving Elliot to wonder when and how she'd make him pay for calling her a sissy.

Chapter 4

Elliot wore a big frown to dinner that evening. He had showered and changed clothes but he still felt icky. He thought about Hannah and sighed, realizing the icky feeling had nothing to do with jumping in the river. It was their fight earlier that was making him feel miserable.

He silently set the kitchen table with three place settings. His mother talked excitedly about a work project she'd finished that day while she removed a large casserole dish from the oven filled with chicken and rice. Lost in thought, Elliot didn't hear a word she said.

Professor Brown tapped on the back door and walked into the kitchen carrying a bowl filled with a mixed vegetable salad. He often shared meals with Elliot and his parents since moving to Cypress Springs last year and buying the house next door. Grandma Brown had died when Elliot was little and he hardly remembered her.

The professor studied Elliot's face. "Sounded like you and Hannah were having quite an argument this afternoon outside the workshop," he said gently as he set the bowl on the table and removed the plastic wrap from the top of it. "Everything okay with you two?"

Elliot looked back and forth at the concerned faces of his grandfather and mother. Being an only child was like living under a magnifying glass – no place to hide, he thought. How he envied Miguel who had two older sisters and Hannah who had three older brothers and one younger brother. He was sure they got away with more stuff just because their parents had to spread their attention so thin.

He commanded his face to grin and made a silly face, hoping to make them smile. "We were just goofing around. Let's eat. I'm starving," he said, eager to change the subject.

Elliot actually was very hungry. He ate quickly, only half listening to the adults chat about the weather and his grandpa's appointment to see an eye doctor coming up on Friday. Then Professor Brown starting telling his mom about the reporter who had interviewed him that afternoon.

That caught Elliot's attention. "Does your Cloud Juicer really work?" he asked, looking at his grandfather intently. "Can Cloud Juice do all those things that lady said, like make you stronger?"

The professor turned his attention to Elliot and thought for a moment before answering. "I'm still working on that project, Elliot. Right now I'm not sure what the effects of Cloud Juice will be. A good scientist doesn't make claims without proof."

That's when Elliot knocked over his glass, drowning the peas from the salad he had intentionally left on his plate and sending a river of milk across the table. The milk fell like raindrops over the edge of the tablecloth. Elliot and his mother both scrambled for paper towels to clean up the mess, but Elliot tripped over Crocket who was lapping up the milk. Elliot landed with a thump and slid across the wet floor into his mother's legs. She lost her balance and sat down hard.

They looked at each other in silence. Elliot's mother started to giggle. Then she started to laugh, which made Elliot giggle. Then they both laughed so hard, tears rolled down their cheeks. The milk continued to drip, drip, drip from the table above them. For a few minutes anyway, Elliot forgot about his problems with Hannah and Field Day.

But midnight found Elliot still tossing and turning in his bed. He simply could not fall asleep. Cloud Juice . . . Hannah . . . his dad's broken camera . . . a white picket fence . . . Field Day . . . a blue ribbon . . . Cloud Juice again. Elliot's thoughts shifted and swirled like the cloud formations he and Miguel loved to watch.

"That Hannah thinks she's such a know-it-all," Elliot grumbled, rolling out of bed and grabbing a pair of blue jeans he had tossed over a chair earlier. He was going to take a closer look at the Cloud Juicer. Maybe smell the Cloud Juice. Nothing wrong with that, Elliot thought as he pulled a T-shirt over his head.

He carried his sneakers as he crept down the stairs and headed for the back door. If his mother woke up, he'd explain that he was having trouble sleeping and that he was going to the kitchen for a glass of milk. It was true that he was having trouble sleeping but right now Elliot was more interested in drinking Cloud Juice than milk.

Elliot sat down on the top step of the back porch to tie his shoes and glanced over at Crocket sleeping on his big, fluffy, cedar chip pillow – his favorite bed when the weather was mild like it was tonight. Crocket opened his eyes and lifted one ear when he saw Elliot on the porch, but showed no interest in following him.

A low ground fog covered the yard; a half moon peeked out from fast, highflying clouds above. Elliot started out slowly across the yard toward the workshop, glancing nervously around him. The patio furniture looked like giant, killer insects waiting to pounce on him in the dark mist. He hurried on. The gate between the two yards creaked slightly as Elliot opened it to pass through.

Was that still his grandfather's warm, inviting workshop or had it become an evil monster's laboratory in the night? Elliot gulped and stepped forward. A small light on his grandfather's back porch barely illuminated the front door of the workshop. He turned the doorknob and was surprised to find the little building locked.

Elliot walked around the side of the workshop and spotted a window that was open a couple inches. He stepped up on an overturned bucket, pulled off the screen and pushed upward on the window as hard as he could. It didn't budge.

"I need help," Elliot muttered softly. "I need Miguel and Hannah – well at least Miguel." Usually Hannah was right in the middle of their adventures. "Why is she being so stupid about this?" he asked himself in frustration.

Just then something cold and moist pressed against Elliot's hand. He spun around so fast he slipped off the bucket and hit the grass with a thud. "Crocket, you scared me so bad, I almost wet my pants," Elliot whispered loudly to the dog. "How did you get over here anyway?" he asked quietly, grabbing Crocket's collar.

As they hurried back across the grass toward Elliot's yard, he noticed the gate was slightly open. He was sure he'd closed it on his way over to his grandfather's workshop.

Elliot slinked back into his house and up to his room as fast as he could without making any noise. He'd had enough adventure for one night but he was more determined than ever to get the Cloud Juice. He decided it must be very powerful stuff if his grandfather kept the workshop locked at night. "Miguel just has to help me get into the workshop tomorrow night," Elliot muttered quietly.

A gentle breeze stirred the curtains hanging by the open window in his bedroom as he dozed off. Meanwhile, a tall, dark figure stepped out of the shadows near Professor Brown's house. The person walked quickly down the street and got into the passenger side of a car waiting there. The engine turned and the car rolled slowly down the street. At the end of the block, its headlights flashed on and the car sped away.

Chapter 5

"There's Hannah up ahead," Miguel said to Elliot the next morning as he came riding up to the Brown front yard on his bike. "Let's catch up with her." The three of them almost always either walked or rode their bikes to school together since it was only four blocks away.

Elliot, who was pushing his bike through the gate, had seen Hannah too. " Wait up Miguel. I've gotta tie my shoe." After his bitter fight with Hannah the afternoon before, Elliot wasn't about to risk getting clobbered by her this early in the day. He propped his bike against the newly painted white picket fence and dawdled over tying one of his sneakers, giving Hannah plenty of time to get ahead of them.

"Hurry up, we'll be late," Miguel said impatiently as he squirmed on his bicycle seat. Several other students had already passed by them while Elliot fooled around with his shoestrings.

"All right, all right." Elliot grabbed his bike. They were just rolling by his grandfather's house when the professor greeted them as he walked out of his front door.

"Morning boys," Professor Brown said brightly. He was dressed in khaki slacks, a blue striped shirt and a bright, red tie. He swung his briefcase as he walked toward them, looking cheerful as usual. He must be teaching at the college today, Elliot thought.

"Good Morning Professor Brown," Miguel said with a wave of his hand.

"Hey, grandpa," Elliot said, smiling

"How are you two partners in crime today?" the professor asked, waiting for them to pass before he continued walking to his car parked at the curb in front of his house. "Say, Elliot," the professor called after them, pausing as he opened his car door. The boys stopped and looked back at him. "Did you or your mother hear any unusual noises outside your house during the night?"

Elliot's stomach did a flip-flop. "I don't remember hearing anything and mom didn't say anything this morning about waking up during the night."

Elliot was telling the truth. He hadn't heard any noises during the night; he was the one who had been making them. His grandfather must have heard him after Crocket surprised him while trying to sneak into the workshop.

"Um . . . ah . . . what did you hear?" The palms of Elliot's hands were sweaty.

"Thought I heard some commotion in the backyard near the workshop . . . probably just raccoons," his grandfather said thoughtfully. "You boys better get going or you'll be late for school."

Elliot and Miguel had to race all the way to school to get there before the last bell rang. Their footsteps echoed down the empty hallway and they were the last students to arrive at their classroom.

"What was your grandpa talking about?" Miguel gave Elliot a suspicious look.

"I'll explain later." They walked to opposite corners of the room. Within the first week of the school last fall, their teacher, Mrs. Holland, had moved Elliot, Miguel and Hannah as far apart as she possibly could.

They thought that separating the three of them had been horribly unfair of her. But today Elliot was glad to be sitting as far away from Hannah as possible. He had to walk by her on his way to his desk but she pretended not to even notice him. Fine with me, Elliot thought grumpily.

Mrs. Holland started their science lesson in late morning. "Today we're going to begin our chapter on clouds and precipitation," she said in her energetic voice. "Can anyone tell me what clouds are?"

Miguel waved his right arm wildly in the air. Mrs. Holland pointed a plump finger at him and said, "Yes, Miguel."

"Clouds are whatever you want them to be," he said excitedly. "Battle ships . . . dragons . . . gigantic hot fudge sundaes." The class erupted in laughter. "Sheep . . . alien space ships . . . monsters," he continued on, trying to talk over the noise of his classmates.

Mrs. Holland's round shoulders shook with laughter too. She brushed a loose strand of her long, curly, black hair from her face and said, "Okay . . . quiet everyone. Miguel is right. We can imagine clouds to be all kinds of things but right now I want us to imagine that we are scientists who study the weather. Clouds are actually made up of tiny droplets of water."

The teacher continued on with the lesson and Elliot soon drifted away, sleepy from his late night escapade and hypnotized by his teacher's monotonous voice in the background saying, "Blah, blah, blah."

"Now look in your books. Can anyone name one type of cloud and describe it for us?" Mrs. Holland asked hopefully. She looked around the room as several students raised their hands, eager to answer her question. She pointed to the back of the room to a red headed, freckled-faced boy name Justin.

"Kirrus," he said uncertainly.

"Sir-es," the teacher corrected him gently. "C-i-r-r-u-s is pronounced with the soft 'c' sound. Please describe cirrus clouds Justin."

The boy read from his book. "Cirrus clouds are white, feathery clouds usually seen during fair weather. They are so high in the air that they are made of tiny bits of ice."

Mrs. Holland smiled. "Excellent. Who else?" She spotted Elliot staring out of the window and walked slowly toward that side of the room.

She called on Rosa, a tiny girl with enormous, brown eyes, who sat at the front of the room near the teacher's desk. Rosa blushed and started to read. "Cumulus clouds look like domes of fluffy cotton. You see them during fair weather but they can bring rain."

"Thank you Rosa." Mrs. Holland walked over to stand by Elliot's desk, blocking his view. "Elliot?" she said loudly.

Elliot shot straight up in his desk, suddenly aware that everyone was staring at him. "Ma'am?" His stomach was doing gymnastics again.

"Clouds, Elliot?" Mrs. Holland crossed her solid arms and waited for him to answer.

He stared at her blankly, his brain still in a fog. "Cloud Juice?" he asked in amazement. How could she possibly know about his grandfather's invention?

"What are you talking about?" Mrs. Holland asked in a puzzled voice. "I know about rain water and dew drops and snow flakes, but I've never heard of Cloud Juice." Elliot's classmates snickered while he sank as far as he could into his chair. "Now back to our lesson. Follow along in your books and pay attention." She gave Elliot a stern look. He thought his face would melt in embarrassment.

Mrs. Holland continued. "Hannah tell us about the third type of cloud, please."

Hannah spoke very quietly and made a point of not looking over at Elliot. "Low, gray clouds spread across the sky that can bring rain are called stratus clouds."

"Very good, Hannah," Mrs. Holland said and she went on to talk about different forms of precipitation like rain, hail, sleet and snow.

Elliot was relieved when the teacher announced they would begin an experiment in evaporation. That'll make everyone forget about my dumb stunt, he thought. And he was right. The room buzzed with activity as students moved their desks together to form groups of four at Mrs. Holland's request. Cory Stone accidentally spilled a glass of water down the back of Bethany Mason's blouse, or so he claimed. So, the quick-thinking Mrs. Holland made Bethany part of the evaporation experiment. All eyes were on Bethany as the teacher dried her blouse, which she still wore, with a hair dryer, showing how heat and wind can speed up evaporation. Elliot was happy to be out of the spotlight.

When Mrs. Holland announced that it was lunchtime, Elliot squeezed behind Miguel in the line forming at the door. "I have a favor to ask," Elliot whispered as they started moving out into the hallway.

He told Miguel about his late night visit to his grandfather's workshop and how he'd gone home empty handed. "I need your help to get the Cloud Juice. Do you think you can stay over at my house tonight?"

"I don't know," Miguel said, sounding unconvinced.

"It'll be fun – like being in a spy movie," Elliot said excitedly. "We'll pretend we're secret agents." Miguel's face brightened and he nodded in agreement.

The two boys were talking so intently they didn't notice Hannah at first. She had slipped up behind them in line and overheard them talking about their plans for that night.

"Hey you two," she said, acting as though nothing had happened the day before. Elliot expected Hannah to tease him about getting caught not paying attention in class, but she didn't say a word.

"Oh, hi," they both stammered, but immediately clammed up about what they were planning to do later. Fortunately, the line moved ahead and they reached the lunch counter. Their attention turned to food. Miguel chattered away and told jokes while the three of them ate lunch together but neither Hannah or Elliot had much to say. They were both glad when it was time to go back to their classroom. Later, Hannah watched Elliot and Miguel hurry away from school on their bicycles, talking excitedly to each other.

"Ha, I'll show them," Hannah said with a big frown on her face as she watched her friends disappear down the street.

Chapter 6

All the way home from school, the boys tried to think up a good excuse for Miguel to stay overnight at Elliot's house. Usually their mothers wouldn't allow a sleepover on a school night. They didn't want to lie to their mothers but they couldn't tell them they were planning a burglary either.

They arrived in front of the Brown house just as Elliot's mother jogged up to the gate. Janet Brown had her blond hair tied up in a ponytail and droplets of sweat dotted her forehead. She leaned over to stretch her legs as she greeted the boys.

Elliot and Miguel both started talking at once. Elliot's mother stood up and listened to them with an amused look on her face.

"Mrs. Brown, it's really important that I stay overnight at your house tonight."

"I need Miguel's help with a science project . . . It's something we have to do in the dark and I can't do it without Miguel . . . please . . . please."

"It's life or death," Miguel ended dramatically. They paused and looked at her hopefully.

"Really? In the dark . . . life or death? Must be some school project," she said with a look of disbelief. She returned to stretching her legs.

"Um . . . life or death . . . because it's something I have to do before school starts tomorrow," Elliot said. "Too bad dad's not here to help me," he added softly, looking down at his feet and sighing. His mother looked guilt-stricken. Elliot really did miss his father but at the moment he was simply trying to get his mother's sympathy. It worked.

"Elliot, you know I don't think having your friends stay overnight on a school night is a good idea but this might work out really well. I want to go to a lecture at the college with your grandpa but I don't want to leave you home alone. Maybe you can have dinner with Miguel's family and then he can spend the night with us," she said. "Let me call his mother and we'll see."

Luck was on their side – so far anyway. Their mothers agreed that Elliot would have dinner with the Sanchez family and Miguel would spend the night with the Browns. Elliot was thrilled. In just a short time, he would have the Cloud Juice he needed to drink so he could be a winner at Field Day. They passed the time until dinner in Miguel's tree house, talking wildly about the adventure they were plotting for later that night. Neither of them would admit it, but they both missed Hannah.

Just when Elliot and Miguel thought they were about to die from hunger, Miguel's mother called up to them in the tree house, "Anybody up there want to go eat pizza?" Elliot and Miguel practically fell over each other trying to be the first one down to the ground. They raced for the Sanchez's minivan parked in the driveway where Miguel's dad was waiting behind the steering wheel.

"Hi boys," Dr. Sanchez said. "How's Crocket doing?" He glanced at Elliot in the rearview mirror, a broad smile lighting up his handsome face. Miguel's father was a veterinarian who had given Crocket his shots a few weeks earlier.

"Okay," Elliot said shyly. Miguel's mom got into the minivan and they started down the street. It would be just the four them going out for pizza since one of Miguel's sisters was babysitting and the other one was visiting at a friend's house.

"Look, there's Hannah," Miguel said excitedly. They waved at Hannah as they drove by her, but she was staring down at the sidewalk as she walked and didn't notice them.

Dr. Sanchez had to drive around the town square in downtown Cypress Springs twice before finding a parking spot and they ended up walking a half block to Mamma Bubba's Pizza. Miguel begged for quarters so he and Elliot could play arcade games while they waited to eat. Mamma Bubba's was busy for a Tuesday night and it seemed to take forever for their pizzas to be ready.

"27 . . . that's our number," Miguel said breathlessly. The boys followed Dr. Sanchez up to the counter to pick up their pizzas and then rushed back to their table. The larger of the two pizzas was their favorite – the Road Kill Special with every kind of meat on the menu and a sprinkling of hot chili peppers and onions. The small vegetarian pizza was for Miguel's petite mother. Just as the boys started to attack the steaming pizza, they heard their names.

"Hi Elliot . . . Hi Miguel," said a soft, teasing feminine voice. They looked up at the same time, their mouths hanging open, the slice of pizza they were each holding suspended in mid-air. The woman's arrival saved them from burning their mouths.

"Hello, I'm Paula Ripkin," the woman said to Miguel's parents who returned her greeting with puzzled smiles. Miguel stared at her in complete adoration.

"She's a famous writer who is going to write a story about Elliot's grandpa," he said reverently. The woman's cheeks turned slightly pink.

"Well, I wouldn't say I'm a famous writer but I do write for a health magazine and I met Miguel and Elliot while I was interviewing Professor Brown yesterday," she explained in her bubbly voice.

"Really? What magazine do you write for?" asked Mrs. Sanchez with genuine interest. "I manage the health food store here in town and I think I read all the health magazines," she added with a dainty laugh.

"Um . . . ah . . . well . . . I'm sure it's one you've never heard of before. Actually, we're just getting it started," she stammered. She quickly turned to face Elliot. "Anyway . . . Elliot, I forgot to ask your grandfather a question yesterday. I called him on the telephone a little while ago, but he didn't answer. Do you know when he'll be home?"

Elliot had just taken a big bite of pizza so it took him a minute to answer her question. "I'm not sure . . . I guess around 8:00. He and my mom went to something at the college," he replied, still chewing on his pizza.

A loud voice from behind the pizza counter called out, "34!"

"Gotta run . . . that's my number," the writer exclaimed, lighting up the table one more time with her blinding smile. "So nice to meet you. Bye, boys," she added before picking up her pizza-to-go and hurrying out the door.

Chapter 7

Actually, it was closer to 8:30 that evening when Janet Brown knocked on the front door of the Sanchez house, ready to pick up Elliot and Miguel. "Sorry I'm so late," she apologized to Miguel's mother as she waved goodbye.

She turned to the two boys. "Are you sure you two are still going to have time to work on a school project tonight?" she asked Elliot with concern in her voice.

"Oh sure lots . . . can you carry Miguel's sleeping bag?" Elliot and Miguel bounced down the sidewalk ahead of her. Tree limbs swayed and creaked as a sudden gust of wind swept down the street; thunder rumbled in the distance.

A ringing telephone greeted them as they walked in the door and Elliot made a dash to the kitchen to answer it. "Hello?" he said, while scratching Crocket's head.

"Hi, Elliot." His dad's voice boomed over the telephone. "Where've you been? This is the third time I've called tonight. Anything new happening at home? Are you being good? I miss you."

Elliot wasn't about to answer the last two questions. He couldn't explain about the Cloud Juice over the telephone. His dad wouldn't understand. And he certainly wouldn't approve of what he and Miguel were planning on doing later that night.

"Miss you too, dad . . . gotta go. MOM," he yelled even though she was standing a few feet away. "It's dad."

While his mother was busy talking on the telephone, Elliot rummaged around the utility room until he found a small flashlight. They would need it later to sneak into his grandfather's workshop. Then he and Miguel grabbed a bag of potato chips and a couple of sodas and ran up the stairs to Elliot's room and closed the door.

A short time later his mother knocked on the door. "Do you need any help with your project? I know I'm not as good at science as your dad but I'll give it a try," she said half-heartedly.

Elliot yelled through the door in a panic. "No . . . thanks, mom. We're doing okay."

"I'm going to sleep then. Don't stay up too late," she called to them in a drowsy voice. "Good night."

"Good night," Elliot said loudly. "We'll have to wait awhile before we can sneak over to the workshop," he added very quietly to Miguel, who had climbed into his sleeping bag. Elliot flopped onto his bed.

The boys found themselves getting sleepy while they waited so they turned off the overhead light and scared each other with ghost stories they'd heard at summer camp. They took turns holding the flashlight under their chins so that the beam of light made them look like ghouls sitting in the dark.

"*. . . and so Johnny decided to take a shortcut through the graveyard, trying to get away from some bad men who were chasing him. It was really dark and he stumbled over a shovel* *and fell into a freshly-dug grave and screamed in terror. He could hear the bad men getting closer but he couldn't climb out of the hole. Then a pale, white hand reached down into the grave at him. Johnny screamed again. A scratchy voice said, 'Don't be afraid.' The hand grabbed his shoulder and pulled him out of the grave and dropped him onto the ground. Johnny saw a ghost floating above him who was at least ten feet tall. The ghost zoomed in close to his face. His breath was cold as ice and it smelled like moldy cheese. 'Never come here again,' the ghost warned him. Johnny trembled with fear. 'No . . . I won't . . . thanks for helping me.' Then he jumped up and ran home as fast as he could, too afraid to look back. The next day, no one would believe his story but the two men who were chasing him were never seen again.*" Miguel ended his story in a whisper.

Both Elliot and Miguel jumped as a flash of lightning filled the room, followed quickly by a loud clap of thunder that rattled the house.

"Maybe going over to your grandpa's workshop tonight isn't such a great idea," Miguel said, sinking down farther into his sleeping bag. "Why don't you just ask him if you can have some of the Cloud Juice tomorrow?" he suggested hopefully.

The ghost stories and the storm had spooked Elliot too but suddenly winning an event at Field Day had become the most important thing in his life

"We've gotta do it tonight. Field Day is only a couple days away and it will take time for the Cloud Juice to start working." Elliot pleaded, "C'mon . . . this will be fun . . . just like being in a scary movie."

Reluctantly, Miguel followed Elliot down the hall. They froze when they heard Elliot's mother cough as they walked by her open bedroom door. They waited until she settled back to sleep and then hurried down the stairs, making a beeline for the kitchen. There they found Crocket nervously pacing back and forth. Crocket didn't like thunderstorms so Mrs. Brown had moved him inside for the night. He wagged his tail and whimpered when he saw the boys.

"Shhh." Elliot tried to calm the dog. "Stay . . . stay," he whispered as he slowly opened the back door and he and Miguel slipped out onto the back porch. The wind was growing stronger, whipping the large pecan trees in the backyard around wildly.

Elliot decided to turn on the flashlight to make sure it was still working, but another flash of lightning made it almost impossible to see the tiny beam of light. Thunder boomed overhead.

Then from out of the darkness a large, white shape came sailing toward them. Both Elliot and Miguel took a big step backward as it came closer. "It's just a plastic bag," Miguel said with a nervous laugh. The bag blew past them and caught on a low hanging branch, fluttering and flapping in the wind.

"It'll only take a minute to get the Cloud Juice and we'll come right back," Elliot said, turning to his friend. "Let's go!"

Miguel nodded silently and the two of them raced across the yard toward Professor Brown's workshop. The wind almost ripped the garden gate out of Elliot's hand. He struggled to close it again and they hurried on to the workshop, which was suddenly outlined by another flash of lightning.

"C'mon. We have to go around to the side of the workshop . . . there's a window that's open," Elliot said as he continued to walk.

"No, we don't," Miguel replied as he stared at the front of the workshop.

"Yes, we do," Elliot said impatiently but he turned around and walked back to stand by his friend. Miguel had picked a bad time to be stubborn.

"No, we don't. See . . . the door's open," Miguel said, pointing at the front of the building. Another gust of wind yanked the door open wider. As they hurried inside the workshop, Elliot pulled it closed behind him.

Lightning lit up the sky once again. Elliot and Miguel couldn't believe their eyes. "Look at the mess," Miguel exclaimed. Elliot scanned the room with his flashlight. Plants had been knocked over and potting soil was scattered everywhere. Broken glass and paper littered the floor.

"I don't like this . . . we're gonna get in trouble," Miguel said, shaking his head from side to side. He stayed by the door while Elliot walked toward the back of the workshop.

"Maybe grandpa didn't close the door all of the way and wind blew it open. Then raccoons or squirrels got in and accidentally knocked all this stuff down," replied Elliot, sounding a lot braver than he felt. It was a story he wanted to believe.

Using his flashlight to help him find his way in the dark, Elliot found the table where his grandfather's Cloud Juicer machine had been setting the day before. A shiver of excitement ran through him when he discovered a rack of corked test tubes each marked Cloud Juice that was almost hidden behind a stack of books. "Come see what I've found," he cried out. He grabbed two of the test tubes, sliding one of them into his pants pocket.

Miguel raced over to join him. "You found it? Let's go." He said shakily.

Elliot opened the top of one of the test tubes and sniffed the clear liquid. "It doesn't have a smell."

"Great. Let's get out of here." Miguel tugged at Elliot's arm.

"The Cloud Juice can't hurt me if it's not killing grandpa's plants. It's not like I'm really taking drugs. I just want to do something really great to impress mom and dad for once," Elliot jabbered on trying to overcome his guilt.

"Can we talk about this when we get back to your house?" Miguel glanced nervously around. The two boys started to walk quickly back to the entrance of the workshop.

"Did you hear that noise?" The wind had settled down as the storm passed quickly by; thunder rumbled off in the distance. They paused to listen.

Then Elliot turned to face Miguel. "I'll just take a sip of the Cloud Juice and if it tastes weird, I'll spit it out," Elliot said. He uncorked one of the test tubes and took a big swig.

Just then, a deep voice called out from the doorway, "Hold it right there."

Chapter 8

Elliot dropped the test tube and whirled around to face the door. Two powerful beams of light instantly blinded him. Oh no, I've swallowed the Cloud Juice, he thought frantically. He glanced over at Miguel who looked like a deer caught in the headlights of an oncoming car, his large brown eyes opened wide in fear.

"Police. Hands in the air," barked one of two uniformed officers as they started toward them. Elliot began to tremble. If he didn't die from drinking the Cloud Juice he would probably spend the rest of his life in prison. Even worse, he had managed to get one of his best friends in trouble. Again.

Another loud voice bellowed from the entrance of the workshop. "What the dickens is going on here?" Professor Brown stepped through the door and flipped on the switch for the overhead lights. He was wearing pajamas and slippers and the hair on back of his head stood straight up from sleeping on it. He carried a baseball bat in one hand. The professor looked around in amazement at Elliot and Miguel and at the two police officers who had spun around and were now pointing guns at him. Then he noticed that his workshop was completely topsy-turvy.

"Why did you do this, Elliot?" his grandfather demanded with more sadness than anger in his voice, dropping the baseball bat that suddenly seemed to have become too heavy for him to hold.

"You know these boys?" asked the taller of the two police officers. Both of the officers relaxed when the bat hit the ground.

"This is my grandson and his friend," Professor Brown said with a pained voice.

Elliot walked toward his grandfather. "Honest . . . grandpa. We didn't mess up your workshop," Elliot said softly. "We've only been here a few minutes. The door was open and it looked like this when we got here. Honest." He had never seen his grandfather look at him with such disappointment.

"What were you doing here then?" the other police officer asked suspiciously.

That's when Elliot told a big whopping lie. "I thought I left one of my books in here the other day and I need it for school tomorrow," he stammered. First a burglar, then a thief and now a liar. The knot in Elliot's stomach was growing tighter and tighter.

Then his arms and legs began to tingle. He was short of breath and his ears felt like they were on fire. What if the Cloud Juice is starting to work, Elliot wondered to himself. What if I turn green in front of the police?

Professor Brown swept past Elliot, heading toward the back of the workshop, setting plants upright and gathering up papers from the floor as he walked. From the other side of the room, Professor Brown yelled out loudly, "My Cloud Juicer is missing!"

One of the two police officers hurried over to where Professor Brown was standing. He started writing in a notebook as the professor described his invention, waving his arms in agitation. The other policeman stood silently staring at Elliot and Miguel, who couldn't have looked more miserable.

That's when Elliot's mother walked through the door with Crocket on her heels, shaking her head in disbelief when she saw Elliot and Miguel. "Something woke me up . . . I checked your room and you weren't there," she said, her voice catching in her throat. It hadn't even occurred to Elliot that his mother might check on them during the storm, that finding them missing would worry her. She was blinking very fast to keep back the tears and her face was white as a ghost.

"So this was the life or death project you had to work on in the dark?" Elliot's mother crossed her arms over her chest, looking angrily back and forth at the two boys. Elliot and Miguel started to tell their story all over again and before long everyone was talking at once. Crocket, who was the only one who seemed happy to find the boys in the workshop, started to bark loudly, running around in circles.

"Quiet," the taller of the two policemen shouted out. Everyone became very still. Even Crocket stopped barking and sat politely at attention. "If you claim your invention is missing, then maybe these boys are telling the truth after all . . . or at least mostly telling the truth," he added, growling at Elliot and Miguel.

When the police finished asking questions for their report, Professor Brown thought of one to ask, "How did you know there was a burglary going on here? I didn't hear any noise until a short time ago."

"We got a tip from an anonymous caller," one of the police officers replied, looking up from his notebook.

Elliot and Miguel couldn't believe what they had just heard. Their eyes locked in anger and disbelief. "Hannah!" Elliot whispered.

Miguel nodded in agreement. "She must have overheard us talking at lunch and she called the cops and ratted on us," he whispered back dramatically.

It was almost 11:00 when the police finally left. Elliot walked over to stand by his grandfather who was locking the workshop. "I'm sorry grandpa . . ." he started to say.

The professor interrupted him. "We'll talk tomorrow," he said in a tired voice. "Good night." He turned away and walked quickly back toward his house.

"Just wait until your father gets home, Elliot Jonathan Brown." Elliot's mother marched them back home. "And Miguel, what will your parents say when I tell them about this?" Both boys groaned. Elliot was sure he would be grounded until he was 102. The boys stumbled up the stairs to Elliot's bedroom totally exhausted. Their evening of crime had drained every ounce of energy from their bodies. Elliot collapsed onto his bed.

Miguel crawled into a sleeping bag on the floor and sighed. "My parents will never let me stay over at your house again."

Elliot was too tired to say another word but his mind was a jumble of thoughts. Somehow he would just have to make his grandfather and mother believe that he hadn't vandalized the workshop. As he started to doze off to sleep, Elliot remembered the other test tube of Cloud Juice in his pants pocket. He turned onto his side; Miguel appeared to be asleep already.

Elliot climbed out of bed and searched the pockets of his trousers. He held the test tube of Cloud Juice up in the faint light shining into his bedroom window from the streetlight. Is winning at Field Day worth all this trouble, he wondered silently. He remembered the disappointment in his grandfather's eyes and the shock on his mother's face.

No turning back now, he thought stubbornly. Winning will change everything. Elliot hid the Cloud Juice in the back of his closet and crept back into bed as light rain began to tap on his bedroom window. Elliot drifted off to sleep not realizing that his troubles had only just begun.

Chapter 9

"Boys, time to wake up and get ready for school," Elliot's mother yelled from the foot of the stairs in a grumpy voice.

Elliot jumped out bed and glanced down at his feet. "See, none of my toes shriveled up and fell off." Memories from last night's adventure seemed like a distant bad dream but he was certain he had swallowed some of the Cloud Juice.

Miguel looked groggily up at him from his sleeping bag on the floor. Then his eyes opened wide in horror. "Elliot . . . your face . . . you . . . you look like a slimy, green, space alien," he said, choking on the words. Miguel covered his face with a pillow and screamed.

Elliot raced down the hall to the bathroom to look in the mirror, relieved to see he looked the way he always did. "Very funny, buffalo breath," Elliot called out hotly as he zipped back down the hall. Miguel howled with laughter. Elliot attacked him with his pillow. Miguel dodged the blow and bopped Elliot on the head with his pillow. They were in the middle of an intense pillow fight when Mrs. Brown appeared at the bedroom door.

"Elliot!" Her voice cut through the air. Pillows froze in mid-air and the boys turned to look at her. Her pale face looked tired. "Please get dressed right now. You'll be late for school," she said quietly.

"Yes ma'am," both boys stammered. Elliot wanted to say something to make things right with his mother, to make that sad look on her face go away, but he couldn't find the right words.

Elliot and Miguel dressed for school and hurried to the kitchen where they found two glasses of orange juice already poured for them. They gulped down the juice, grabbed a couple of Pop Tarts and headed for the front door.

Just as they were about to walk out the door, Elliot said, "Wait here a minute." He ran back through the kitchen and found his mother in her office at work in front of her computer. Elliot hated mushy stuff like hugs and kisses but he felt so bad he threw his arms around his mother's neck. "I'm really sorry I worried you last night." His mother hugged him back and then held him out at arm's length. She gave him a small smile. "Don't be late for school."

All morning Elliot felt lightheaded. He suspected the Cloud Juice was starting to work when he got every answer right on a math quiz, something that almost never happened to Elliot. But he was convinced of it when Megan Evans, the cutest girl in fourth grade, sat by him at lunch. He wasn't crazy about girls, but girls couldn't resist a superstar like Elliot Brown. It was a fact of life he would just have to get used to.

Before returning to his classroom after lunch, Elliot stopped by the boys' bathroom, glad to find the room empty. He jumped up and down in front of the mirror. Yes, he definitely was jumping higher. He practiced leaping. He was sure he had never leaped so far. The Cloud Juice was nothing short of a miracle.

Elliot couldn't wait for P.E. class to start that afternoon. It would be the last practice before Field Day. "Coach Meadows, would it be all right if I try out for the long jump again today?" he asked eagerly.

The boys gathered around the long jump sandpit to watch him, most of them jeering at Elliot. "Go for it klutz," someone yelled. "You can do it, Elliot," Miguel shouted loudly in support for his friend.

Elliot stepped up to the line and stared hard at the sandpit, trying to concentrate. He took a deep breath and ran as fast as he could. His right foot thumped on the board and as he jumped he remembered to lean forward. He landed hard in the sand and quickly turned around to see how far he had jumped. It seemed like a long way. Coach Meadows and her assistant measured the distance from his footprint to the board.

"11 feet, four inches. Elliot, that's marvelous," she exclaimed, turning to give him a huge smile. "I'm putting your name on the long jump list."

The sneers on his classmates' faces disappeared. A few of the more popular boys who usually ignored Elliot crowded around him, slapping him on the back. Elliot was thrilled. The Cloud Juice had worked. Life was wonderful. When Miguel came over to congratulate him, Elliot turned away from him, focusing his attention on his new buddies instead.

Hannah had walked over to the long jump area to see what all of the excitement was about and saw Elliot snub Miguel. She also saw the scowl on Miguel's face as he turned to leave when the final school bell rang, while Elliot continued to laugh with his newfound fans.

"Well aren't you Mr. Big Stuff," a girl's voice called out to Elliot in a taunting voice as he started to leave the school grounds a few minutes later. He turned to see Hannah come charging up to him.

In his excitement he forgot for a minute how mad she had been at him. "The Cloud Juice really works . . . I'm going to win the long jump on Friday," he said excitedly.

She narrowed her steel gray eyes and shook her head in disbelief. "And that's all that matters to you . . . winning? Being popular? What about your old friends? What about pretending you didn't know Miguel just now?"

Elliot's face turned red with embarrassment, but he would have rather painted a hundred fences than admit that Hannah was right about the way he had acted.

"Oh, like you're such a great friend . . . you traitor," he shot back at her.

"What are you talking about . . . you idiot?" They were back to name-calling.

"You know what I'm talking about. You called the police and told them that Miguel and I were in my grandfather's workshop. It's your fault we got into trouble last night," Elliot shouted at her in anger.

He expected his words to make her really mad. Instead, Hannah became very still; then she quickly turned around and walked away. Were those tears in Hannah's eyes? He had never seen her cry before – not even when she fell off the roof of old Mr. Johnson's garage and scraped both of her knees bloody.

It was a long, lonely walk home from school for superstar Elliot Brown. He had turned his back on Miguel and now he had made Hannah cry. Maybe the Cloud Juice is turning me into a space alien, Elliot thought. He sighed deeply. "No . . . I bet space aliens are a lot nicer to their friends than I am," he mumbled aloud.

Lost in misery, Elliot didn't notice the car following close behind him. Nor did he see it speed away when he opened the gate to his front yard.

Chapter 10

Elliot shot out of bed the next morning like a lit firecracker, determined to talk to Hannah and Miguel before school started and win back their friendship. He dressed quickly and gobbled down a couple pieces of toast before racing out the door and down the sidewalk. Elliot dropped his schoolbag behind a large oak tree half way down the block and waited to ambush his friends. Every couple minutes he peeked around the tree to see if he could spot them, but he almost missed Miguel and Hannah as they hurried past his hiding spot.

"Stop! We have to talk." Elliot jumped out in front of them and blocked their path. His blond hair stood up in spikes and his T-shirt was on inside out. Miguel and Hannah stared at Elliot as though he had gone completely crazy. They said nothing.

"I'm sorry I've been acting so weird this week . . . for saying those mean things . . . for being rude," Elliot said, glancing back and forth at his friends. He stared hard into Hannah's eyes and turned his shoulder to her. "Slug me."

Hannah's eyes opened wide. "I'm not going to hit you," she replied coolly.

"C'mon . . . slug me hard. I deserve it," Elliot insisted.

"NO." Hannah stepped back.

"Well, I will!" Miguel popped Elliot hard on his other shoulder. Elliot yelped in pain, fell to the grass and rolled onto his back. He flailed his arms around wildly and kicked his legs. His tongue hung out of his mouth as he burped loudly. Then Elliot closed his eyes and lay still on the ground.

"Great performance, *amigo*," Miguel said, fighting the urge to laugh at Elliot's silliness. He nudged Elliot's leg gently with his left foot.

"He's so weird," Hannah said with a big smile on her face. "C'mon, let's go Miguel." Hannah winked at Miguel. They walked about twenty feet down the sidewalk and then turned to look back at Elliot who remained perfectly still on the grass.

Miguel's eyes opened wide with concern. "We have to help him . . . call 911 . . ."

Hannah and Miguel rushed back to Elliot and knelt down beside him. "Are you all right?" Hannah asked, leaning close to Elliot. "I must've hit him harder than I thought," Miguel said sadly.

Then Elliot's eyes popped open and he grinned. "Gotcha!" They all screeched with laughter as Miguel held Elliot to the ground and Hannah tickled his ribs. They finally quit rolling around on the grass when the Conroe twins walked past them and sneered. "What babies," Jenny Conroe said with a sniff. They were in sixth grade and thought they were very grown up.

They stood up, out of breath with laughter. Miguel pointed at Elliot. "Your shirt." Elliot looked down and blushed. As he quickly put it on the right way and smoothed down his hair, Elliot stared past Hannah and Miguel. A movement had caught his eye. "There's that man again!" he said excitedly, pointing back toward his house.

"What about him?" Hannah asked curiously. They watched a tall, brown-haired man dressed in a bright, blue jogging suit step into the street. When the stranger stopped to look in both directions to see if any cars were coming, they noticed he was wearing sunglasses even though it was cloudy outside. He walked briskly across the street to the sidewalk and continued on down the block in the opposite direction from them

"Do you know him?" Miguel sounded puzzled.

Elliot explained that the man had stopped by while he had been painting the fence on Saturday and had asked about his grandfather. "I went over to get grandpa so he could talk to him and when we came back, the stranger was gone. Grandpa thought I had made him up. I'm sure that's the same man," Elliot exclaimed, grabbing his schoolbag from the ground.

But the stranger was quickly forgotten as the three of them hurried off to school, chattering and laughing, happy to be friends again. No one said anything about Cloud Juice.

After lunch, the school principal announced over the P.A. system that grades four and five were supposed to file down to the gymnasium for a special presentation. Voices echoed in the large room as each class trooped in noisily and the students lined up in rows on the floor.

Mrs. Woods, the principal, walked into the room with a uniformed police officer who was leading a tan and black German Shepherd dog on a leash. A hush fell over the room.

"Does anyone know what this week has been designated?" Mrs. Woods asked. No one said anything. She continued, "This is Drug Awareness Week and Officer Johnson is here with a special friend to tell you what that means to you."

Sitting in the front row of students between Hannah and Miguel, Elliot squirmed uneasily. Now that he realized what the program was about, he wished he could sneak to the back of the room and hide.

"At least he isn't one of the policemen who caught us in your grandpa's workshop the other night," Miguel said softly to Elliot out of the side of his mouth.

"I bet he knows about us though," Elliot whispered, looking guilty. "They probably sent him here to spy on us."

"Hello," Officer Johnson said. "This is a very special dog named Radar and he has an important job with the police department. Radar has been trained to sniff out drugs." Radar sat down on his haunches in front of Officer Johnson and the dog seemed to stare directly at Elliot.

Officer Johnson talked about how doctors use drugs to help make people well when they are sick. He also warned the students to avoid people who claimed they had drugs to give them that would solve all of their problems.

"That's why Radar and I are here today," he continued. "We want you to understand the difference. If someone tells you that you have to take pills or drink alcohol or else they won't be your friend, what will you say?"

All of the students yelled out in a loud chorus, "No." Elliot shouted just as loudly as the others.

Officer Johnson went on, "If someone tells you that if you take a drug, you'll be funnier or smarter or be better at sports, what will you say?"

Once again, the room rang out with a loud, "No." Elliot's "no" was pretty weak the second time as he thought about drinking the Cloud Juice. Hannah couldn't resist jabbing him in the ribs with her elbow and making a face at him. No one had told Elliot the Cloud Juice would actually help him jump better or run faster. He just knew his grandfather's invention would work. Cloud Juice really isn't a drug, Elliot told himself, but he wished Radar would quit staring at him. He was glad when the program was over and Officer Johnson led the dog away.

Chapter 11

"See you tomorrow at Field Day!" Elliot waved at Hannah and Miguel as they continued past his house after school instead of stopping in like usual. Hannah had to go to a piano lesson and Miguel had to help his mother load their empty aluminum cans, plastic bottles, glass jars and old newspapers into the back of their minivan and take them to the recycling center.

Watching Crocket run toward him reminded Elliot of Radar, the drug dog that had been part of the drug awareness program at school that afternoon. Not only was Elliot still unsure about whether drinking the Cloud Juice was the right thing to do, but he felt miserable whenever he thought about his grandfather. Elliot realized that he hadn't seen or talked to him since he and Miguel had found the professor's workshop vandalized two nights earlier.

Elliot and Crocket ran around the side of the house and stomped up onto the back porch and into the kitchen. Elliot raced over the refrigerator where he grabbed two bottles of apple juice.

"MOM . . . I'm going over to grandpa's."

"Okay, don't slam the door," his mother called back cheerfully from her computer.

SLAM. The back door opened a crack. "Sorry . . . it slipped." Elliot closed the door again, this time gently. As he trotted toward his grandfather's workshop, Elliot scooped up a frisbee from the grass and threw it across the yard for Crocket to catch.

The door to the workshop stood wide open so Elliot went inside expecting to find his grandfather there. Everything was in perfect order. Plants stood neatly in rows on the tables and the floor was swept clean. It seemed as though he had only imagined his adventure with Miguel the other night and the mess they had found in the workshop.

"Grandpa?" Elliot walked to the back of the workshop, looking around. Through an open window he could hear the professor's reply. "Back here, son."

Elliot retraced his steps and walked around to the back of the workshop where he found his grandfather on his knees, happily setting out small tomato plants in his freshly tilled garden. He leaned back and wiped his brow as Elliot handed him a bottle of apple juice. "Thank you!" Professor Brown gave him a big smile. Elliot relaxed and returned the smile. His grandpa wasn't mad at him after all.

"Can I help?" Elliot knelt down and dug into the soil with his hands.

"May I help." His grandfather corrected him and took a sip of juice. "And yes you may. How about planting these green beans for me?" Professor Brown showed Elliot how to dig a shallow, narrow trench, place the seeds a few inches apart and gently cover them with dirt. They worked quietly together for a while, enjoying the sunny, warm afternoon and each other's company. A mockingbird, sitting on the peak of the roof, entertained them with a medley of songs. Crocket stretched out on the grass and dozed off.

"Grandpa, can you come watch me at Field Day tomorrow?" Elliot asked suddenly. Without waiting for his answer, Elliot began to talk excitedly about how well he done in the long jump at school and how he was sure he was going to win a blue ribbon tomorrow.

"Here, let me show you." Elliot had finished planting the row of beans. He stood up and brushed the soil from his knees. Then he ran over to the fence and turned around, staring at the unplanted end of the garden. He ran back as fast as he could, stepped on the edge of the grass by the garden, pretending it was the long jump board and then leaped as far as he could. He landed in the middle of the garden.

"That's fantastic, Elliot!" His grandfather gave him a puzzled look as Elliot came back to sit beside him. "What's with your sudden interest in sports?" Before he knew it, Elliot told his grandfather everything – well, almost everything.

"I just want to win at something so you and mom and dad will be proud of me for a change," Elliot ended in frustration.

His grandfather sighed deeply. "You know, for the last two days I've been trying to figure out what you and Miguel were really looking for in my workshop the other night. Does this wanting to win a blue ribbon have anything to do with Cloud Juice?" his grandfather asked quietly. Elliot didn't answer him and he began to scrape dirt from his sneakers with a twig to avoid returning his grandfather's gaze.

"Let me tell you a story," his grandfather said. "When your dad was about your age . . . well, maybe a little older . . . I guess he was about 14, he decided he needed to have bigger muscles. He was sort of a beanpole like you back then. Anyway, without telling your grandmother or me, your dad ordered this special cream from some magazine that was guaranteed to build up his muscles. He hid it in his closet and every night for a week he rubbed it on his arms and shoulders."

"Did his muscles get really big?" Elliot hung on every word his grandfather said.

His grandfather chuckled. "Nope. He just ended up with a horrible, red, itchy rash. We finally found out what he was doing when your grandmother noticed the rash on his neck."

"Well, then how did he get his muscles?" Elliot asked, picturing his dad's powerful arms.

"After the rash cleared up, your dad spent part of that summer and many more summers helping at his uncle's farm. Hard work and good country food did the job."

They sat quietly for a few minutes and finished drinking their apple juice. Elliot couldn't imagine his father ever being a young boy. He was simply dad.

"Elliot." He heard his mother's voice calling across the yard.

"I guess I better go home. Thanks for letting me help." Elliot started across the yard but suddenly stopped and turned around. "What did that lady forget to ask you?"

Elliot's grandfather shook his head in puzzlement. "You've lost me. What lady?"

"You know, that writer lady who was here the other day. She was at the pizza place the other night when I ate with Miguel and she asked about when you were gonna be home. She said she forgot to ask you something," Elliot said.

"Never heard from her again. Said she and her husband were leaving for California the next day," the professor replied.

Elliot shrugged his shoulders and headed back home. Later that evening after dinner, Elliot called for Crocket to follow him up to his room and closed the door behind them. He opened his closet door and took out the other test tube of Cloud Juice from its hiding place.

He took out the rubber stopper and held up the open tube for Crocket to sniff. The dog didn't seem at all interested in the Cloud Juice and that made Elliot feel better about drinking it.

"But then I guess you haven't been to police school," Elliot said, biting his lip. "Only this one time and I'll never do it ever again. I just really want to win the long jump tomorrow," he said to the dog.

Elliot drank all of the Cloud Juice in the test tube and hid the empty container in his closet again. That night, he didn't sleep well at all. A large, police dog with long fangs chased him through his dreams until early morning.

Chapter 12

Elliot found his mother in the kitchen the next morning. "Good morning," she said with a smile, glancing up from the newspaper she was reading at the table.

"Are you feeling all right?" she added, noticing the dark circles under his eyes. "You've been awfully quiet the last couple days."

"I'm okay," he replied, dodging a kiss on the cheek from her as he poured breakfast cereal and milk into a bowl.

"Your dad is really sorry he can't be here to watch you at Field Day today," his mom said. "He said he'd take us out for hamburgers when he gets home this afternoon. Miguel and Hannah can come along if you'd like and then we can all go play miniature golf," she said, trying to cheer up Elliot.

"That'll be neat." Elliot smiled, hoping now more than ever that later they would be celebrating the blue ribbon he won for the long jump.

Around 8:30 that morning the public high school stadium started filling with students from the Cypress Springs

Elementary School and the two private elementary schools in town. They would be competing in the baseball throw, relay races, 50, 75 and 100-yard dashes, standing broad jump and, of course, the long jump. Most of the students arrived in school buses, but some of them, like Elliot, had driven to the stadium with family members who had volunteered to help

"I'm gonna go find Miguel and Hannah," Elliot said to his mother and grandfather as they got out of the car in the parking lot. Professor Brown had volunteered to help at the snack stand and Elliot's mother had offered to help with the races.

Elliot sped through the entrance of the stadium and then stopped to look over the crowd for his friends. He spotted Hannah standing by a large board that listed all of the Field Day events and the times each grade level would compete. Hannah and her little brother, Mikey, were almost overshadowed by their father, Michael Dawson, who stood next to them. Mr. Dawson, who worked as a firefighter, was a mountain of a man; his bald head and broad shoulders always stood above the crowd. Yet he was a gentle, softhearted man who loved to laugh.

"Hi Hannah. Have you seen Miguel yet?" Elliot said as he trotted over to stand by her. He studied the big event board too and was relieved to see that his long jump competition wouldn't start until 12:30. That would give him time to practice jumping to see if the second dose of Cloud Juice he had drank the night before would give him an extra boost.

Just as Hannah was about to reply, Elliot felt all of the air squeezed out of his lungs as Mr. Dawson gave him a bear hug. "How are you, Elliot?" Mr. Dawson's laugh rang out across the field. He would be announcing events today.

"Fine." Elliot's voice came out as a squeak. He was relieved when Mr. Dawson was called away to announce the start of the Field Day activities and released Elliot from his hold. Hannah's dad was someone who definitely didn't need Cloud Juice, Elliot thought.

"C'mon, let's go. My first race starts in 10 minutes and Miguel said he'd meet us at the starting line," Hannah said excitedly, pointing across the field to where the race would be held. "But first we have to help Mikey find his class." Elliot and Hannah started across the field with her little brother tagging along until they left him with his first-grade teacher.

A small group was already milling around the starting line for the fourth-grade girls' 50-yard dash when Elliot and Hannah walked up. Dressed in a bright gold and purple jogging suit, Miguel was easy to spot.

Miguel flashed a huge smile and started to videotape them as the two approached. "And now here are two of our champion athletes competing today," he said dramatically. "What do you think your chances of winning are today?"

Both of them froze in front of the camera. Hannah giggled. Elliot blushed. Miguel took the camcorder away from his face. "Hey, you're messing up my documentary. Let's try it again."

Miguel turned the camcorder back on. Hannah ran in place while Elliot practiced jumping up and down. Elliot felt like he had springs attached to the bottom of his feet. In fact, he looked to make sure there weren't. He couldn't believe how high he could jump. Miguel laughed. "Now, that's more like it!"

"All fourth-grade girls running the 50-yard dash to the starting line now, please," called out one of the teachers.

"Wish me luck," Hannah said, laughing nervously.

"You don't need luck . . . you always win," Elliot said with a tinge of jealousy. "But I wish you luck anyway," he added quickly.

He and Miguel hurried down to the finish line from where Miguel would videotape the race. A sharp crack sounded and the girls darted down the track toward them. Within a few seconds, Hannah pulled ahead of the other girls and she crossed the finish line a good two feet ahead of the girl who was in second place. The others finished close together.

Hannah collected her blue ribbon and ran over to Elliot and Miguel who both thumped her on the back in congratulations. Miguel videotaped her with her blue ribbon and then the threesome moved on so he could record other events. As the morning went on, Hannah collected two more blue ribbons: one for the 75-yard dash and one for the 100-yard dash. Miguel taped each of the different events as he had promised Coach Meadows he would do.

"I'm starved," Hannah finally exclaimed loudly when it was almost noon.

"Me too," Miguel chimed in. "Let's eat."

They sauntered over to the snack stand where Professor Brown was still volunteering along with two other people. Miguel turned on his camcorder and scanned the booth. "And here is our very own famous Professor Brown selling hot dogs," he said into the microphone of the camcorder.

Elliot's grandfather laughed. "Hey, look at all those blue ribbons you've got," he said, beaming a big smile at Hannah. "And what may I get for you three?"

Miguel and Hannah each ordered a hot dog, potato chips and a large soda. Elliot remained silent. Although his long jump event wouldn't start for at least another half hour, Elliot's stomach was already jumping up and down. A famous grandpa and blue ribbons for Hannah, Elliot thought. Envy pricked at his heart like a sharp needle. "I just have to win at the long jump," he muttered.

"What's that Elliot? I didn't quite hear what you want to eat," Professor Brown said.

"I guess I'll wait until after I do the long jump before I eat anything," Elliot said, hesitantly. "You are going to come watch me, aren't you grandpa?" He looked at his grandfather expectantly.

"I wouldn't miss it for the world, son." Professor Brown waved as the three of them wandered off to find a spot for Miguel and Hannah to eat their lunch.

The announcer called out over the loud speaker that the long jump event for fourth grade boys would begin in five minutes. Elliot jumped up from where he was sitting. "I'm going to get ready. See you over there," he said to his friends as he turned away and walked quickly over to the long jump area.

Elliot was nervous but his heart soared. He practiced jumping up and down a few more times. It seemed he had more bounce in his jump than ever. In just a short time, he would be the winner of the long jump.

Elliot could hear his grandfather's voice booming from the small crowd gathered to watch the long jump. "Come on Elliot, you can do it." Elliot waved and his mother who was standing next to Professor Brown waved back. He saw Miguel with his camcorder and Hannah standing close to the end of the long jump sand pit.

Elliot was the last one in the group of fourth-grade boys to jump. He took a deep breath and ran toward the long jump pit as fast as he could. He knew as soon as his right foot hit the board that his toes were over the edge and when he landed he fell back instead of forward. The short jump would be measured from where his hands hand landed. It didn't matter; the jump wouldn't count anyway because he had stepped over the board.

Cloud Juice or not, there would be no blue ribbon for superstar Elliot Brown today.

Chapter 13

Elliot walked away from the long jump pit in a daze. He had taken the Cloud Juice so he could win a blue ribbon and make his family proud of him but his first jump had been a disaster. He felt like a thief and a loser. Just then, he felt a strong hand squeeze his shoulder. Elliot looked up with tear-filled eyes that were met by his grandfather's gentle blue eyes.

"Grandpa, I took some of your Cloud Juice to help me win today but it's not working," Elliot muttered softly.

"That's what I was afraid of," Professor Brown said. He shook his head sadly. "Do you realize that you could have gotten very sick or even worse from drinking what you thought was Cloud Juice?"

"But it didn't hurt me . . . the Cloud Juice worked at first. I jumped really far at school."

"That's not possible, Elliot." Professor Brown gave him a small smile. "All you drank was plain old rain water I had collected. I haven't actually made any Cloud Juice yet."

Elliot's eyes opened wide. "But it worked . . . it really worked."

"It helped you at first because you sincerely believed it would. But maybe you aren't so sure about the Cloud Juice anymore." Professor Brown tapped his finger to the side of his head. "The imagination is amazingly powerful."

Coach Meadows called for Elliot to hurry back for his second jump. He glanced over his shoulder at his grandfather as he trotted back to the starting line. His grandfather gave him two thumbs up. "You can do this Elliot!"

Elliot took his position. He closed his eyes, took a deep breath and saw himself floating over the sand pit like a cloud. He opened his eyes and ran as fast as he had done the first time. Elliot's right foot landed squarely on the board and then he jumped as far as he could. He fell forward and landed far into the sand pit.

Miguel and Hannah rushed over to stand by Elliot while the coaches measured his jump. Elliot crossed his fingers. "11 feet, five inches," Coach Meadows called out. She turned and smiled at Elliot. "Congratulations, you placed third."

Miguel videotaped Elliot with his yellow ribbon while Hannah clapped. Professor Brown and Elliot's mother hurried over. "I'm so proud of you, Elliot. I can't wait for your dad to see your ribbon," his mother said excitedly.

Elliot hadn't said a word. His face showed no emotion. "But I didn't win . . . I didn't get the blue ribbon," he said flatly

Hannah moved directly in front of Elliot. "You are such a dummy," she exclaimed in frustration. "Have you ever won a ribbon before?"

"No." Elliot scowled at her. He wasn't in the mood for one of Hannah's lectures.

"Did you win a ribbon today?"

"Yes . . . I guess I did win a ribbon!" Elliot was quiet for a moment and then he started to smile.

"So what if it wasn't a blue ribbon." Hannah returned Elliot's smile

"And you did it all on your own." Professor Brown winked at Elliot.

"Yes I did," Elliot said, a grin lighting up his face. All of the guilt he had been feeling about sneaking around with the Cloud Juice lifted from his shoulders. "Let's eat. I'm starved," he said.

Elliot, Hannah and Miguel raced ahead of Professor Brown and Elliot's mother to the snack stand. Field Day was starting to wind down and volunteers had begun to pack away the food, but they were still able to order hot dogs and sodas. Low, dark stratus clouds rolled across the sky, covering the sun and a sudden gust of wind yanked up the canopy of the snack stand, sending paper plates flying everywhere. Flags and banners decorating the stadium that had hung limply during the hot humid morning now snapped in the stiff, cool breeze.

Hannah's father hurried over to them, looking worried. "It sounds like we have some bad weather coming in. It's already raining very hard west of here." He looked at Hannah. "I've been called in to work at the fire station. Since school is dismissed for the day, I'm taking Mikey home. You need to come on too."

"We were going to go over to Elliot's and watch Miguel's movie . . . please, dad," Hannah pleaded.

"It's alright with me," Elliot's mother said. "I was going to ask if Hannah and Miguel could join us for dinner anyway."

Mr. Dawson reluctantly agreed and walked quickly away with Mikey bouncing alongside of him. Hannah ran after them. "Dad . . . take my ribbons home . . . please."

Thunder rumbled in the distance as Elliot and his friends all piled into the back seat of his mother's car. His grandfather rode in the front seat with his mother.

As they turned onto the street from the stadium parking lot, huge raindrops began to splatter on the windshield and Mrs. Brown turned on the car's wipers and headlights so she could see the road ahead. The thick clouds overhead made it seem strangely dark for early afternoon and everyone was quiet while they drove to Elliot's house.

As Mrs. Brown turned on to Austin Street she said, "I'm going to drop you kids off at our house and then drive Elliot's grandfather to the eye doctor's office. They have to put special drops in his eyes, so he can't drive himself. It shouldn't take long so we'll be home in just a bit."

She stopped the car at the curb in front of the house and turned around to look at Elliot, Miguel and Hannah. "Please bring Crocket into the house right away. He won't like being outside in this stormy weather and then I want all of you to stay inside . . . and don't tear the house apart." She and Professor Brown smiled and waved at them and they drove off.

Elliot called for Crocket as he ran across the yard and around the back of the house. Hannah raced ahead of him but Miguel followed more slowly trying to protect his camcorder from the rain.

"Crocket . . . here Crocket," Elliot called again and again. Hannah called for the dog too but they couldn't find Crocket anywhere. "I hope he didn't run away because he was afraid of the storm." Elliot was starting to worry.

"Maybe your mom forgot she left him in the house," Miguel said hopefully from the back porch. It was raining harder now and Elliot and Hannah were getting soaked. They filed through the back door into the kitchen to find

Crocket happily munching away on an entire box of milk biscuits that were scattered all over the floor.

"How did you get that box down from the shelf? You are in so much trouble Crocket Jonathan Brown," Elliot mimicked his mother's voice which made Hannah and Miguel giggle. They continued to laugh as they gathered up the dog treats while Crocket ran around the kitchen trying to eat as many as he could.

Then they heard a harsh voice that made them freeze in their places. "Not nearly as much trouble as you are in." They looked up to see the curly red-haired woman who had interviewed Professor Brown walk toward them holding a pistol in her hand.

Chapter 14

"Give me that thing before you hurt someone with it." A tall, brown-haired man walked into the kitchen behind the woman and grabbed the gun from her hand. He shoved it into his jacket pocket.

"Hey . . . you're the guy who asked me about my grandfather while I was painting the fence. We saw you walking down the sidewalk the other morning," Elliot said in confusion.

"And you're not really a famous writer." Miguel looked at the woman in disbelief.

"Told you so," Hannah crowed.

"Smart kids. Now all of you in the living room where we can keep an eye on you," the man barked at them. Elliot, Hannah and Miguel followed the woman out of the kitchen with the man right behind them.

"Some guard dog you are." Elliot shook his head at Crocket who followed along, wagging his tail in delight. Crocket loved parties and this was turning out to be a wild one. Elliot couldn't believe his eyes when they walked into the living room. Sofa cushions and books from the shelves were scattered on the floor. A lamp had been knocked over and videotapes and DVDs from the entertainment center were thrown around the room. Through the archway, Elliot could see into the dining room. Dishes and table linens had been pulled out of cabinets and drawers and tossed carelessly on the table.

"My mother is going to have a heart attack when she sees this," Elliot said in a hushed voice. The whole situation seemed so unreal that Elliot could imagine his mother giving these two burglars a lecture about the "consequences for their actions."

"We've wasted enough time in this boring, little town," the woman snarled. She walked over to Elliot and leaned close to his face. "Tell us where you've hidden it."

"Hidden what?" Elliot stepped back from the angry woman.

"Don't play dumb. Tell us where the Cloud Juicer is," the man snapped at him.

"How should I know where it is?" Elliot asked. "It was missing the other night when we found my grandpa's workshop all messed up."

The man sneered at Elliot. "We know. We were the ones who tore it up looking for the Cloud Juicer. But we couldn't find it and just as we were leaving, we saw you and your little buddy coming, so we called the cops and reported a burglary so you'd take the blame."

"YOU called the police," Elliot and Miguel shouted as they turned to look at Hannah. "I'm so sorry . . . we thought you did it," Elliot said sadly.

"How sweet . . . now back to business," the man said coldly. "Where is the Cloud Juicer? I saw you snooping around the workshop the night before we broke in so I know you were trying to get it."

"Honest . . . I don't know where it is," Elliot said nervously.

Hannah said very quietly. "I took it."

Everyone turned to her in surprise and said in unison, "YOU took it!"

Hannah looked at Elliot. "I sneaked over to your grandfather's workshop after school on Tuesday and took it so you wouldn't drink the Cloud Juice."

Elliot realized that Hannah had been genuinely concerned about his safety. She believed the Cloud Juice would make him sick the way illegal drugs had made her brother sick. Now, he regretted his unkind words during their argument even more.

"So where did you put the Cloud Juicer," the woman said shrilly, grabbing Hannah by the shoulders and shaking her. Hannah pulled away from her grasp and narrowed her eyes. The two boys jumped to Hannah's side.

Miguel raised his fist to the woman. "Hey, you leave her alone," he shouted.

"My mother and grandfather will be home any minute," Elliot yelled.

The man and woman looked at each other anxiously. "The kid may be telling the truth," she said with a groan. "You said there wasn't going to be any trouble getting this Cloud Juicer and now look at the mess we're in." She tapped the long, blood-red fingernails of one of her hands on the top of the television while running her other hand through her hair in frustration.

"If I show you where the Cloud Juicer is, will you go away and leave us alone?" Hannah asked.

"Where is it?" Both the man and woman demanded as they walked over to her.

"I hid it in our secret hiding place on the island at the city park," Hannah said slowly.

"No way . . . the secret hiding . . . " Elliot started to say when Miguel stepped down hard on his foot and interrupted him.

"Of course, the secret hiding place," Miguel said, playing along with Hannah.

Elliot finally caught on to the game they were playing and chimed in. "Pretty clever . . . I would never have thought of looking for it there."

The man walked quickly over to the window and looked outside to see if anyone was approaching the house. The sky was still dark and gloomy but the rain had let up and it was only sprinkling. "All right, we'll all go to this island of yours but no funny stuff if you want to live to blow out the candles on your next birthday cake," the man said gruffly, patting the bulge from the gun in his jacket pocket.

Chapter 15

They left the house in single file. Once again, the woman led the way and the man followed. Elliot, Miguel and Hannah were sandwiched between them. The man ordered them into the back seat of a dark sedan with heavily tinted windows. While they could see out of the car windows, no one could see them sitting in the car, so it wouldn't do any good to try to wave for help. Car tires squealed as the woman sped away from the curb while the two adults argued about which route to take to the city park.

"Hannah, is the Cloud Juicer really at the island?" Elliot whispered. "The Cloud Juicer is too big to fit into the hiding spot in the tree."

"No it's not at the island," she replied quietly.

"What are we going to do when we get to the park?" Miguel asked in a panicked voice.

"We're going to do what we always do when the pirates attack us on the island," Hannah said with determination.

Elliot groaned quietly. "We're going to climb a tree and throw pecans at a man holding a gun?"

"Neither of you were coming up with any bright ideas," Hannah said defensively.

The man turned and glared at them. "Pipe down back there."

Just then, a sudden gust of wind rocked the car and the woman slammed on the car brakes to avoid a large, falling, tree limb that almost crashed onto the car. Elliot, Hannah and Miguel jerked forward in their seats; Elliot's head bounced off the back of the front seat like a rubber ball. He closed his eyes, stunned for a moment by the pain. For the first time, Elliot was deeply frightened by what was happening to them. He opened his eyes and saw his fear mirrored in Hannah and Miguel's eyes too.

Elliot forced a smile. "Going to the park was a good idea. We'll think of a way to split up and get away from them," he whispered, nodding toward the front seat.

The car screeched to a halt at the low water crossing over the El Toro River and the woman swore under her breath. The low water crossing sign showed that more than three feet of water was rushing across the street, enough to sweep the car into the river.

"I told you we should have gone over the Grand Avenue Bridge," she barked at the man. She backed up the car and swung it around, speeding through a stop sign.

"Slow down . . . you want to attract the cops?" the man snarled back at her.

"Sorry." Miguel, who was sitting in the middle of the back seat, slid into Hannah as the car swung around and then slid back across the seat and collided with Elliot when the car turned wildly onto the bridge over the El Toro River. The rising river had started to creep up over the island and they looked at each other uneasily. The rain was steady again.

The car slid sideways as they drove down the steep gravel road leading into the city park but the woman was able to straighten it back out and she continued on until they were close to the river. She parked by a clump of tall bushes where the car would be hidden from view from the park entrance.

"All right, let's go," the man said, turning to look into the back seat. "We'll follow you, and remember – no funny stuff."

The woman's high-heeled shoes sank into the mud when she got out of the car. "Look . . . just look. My shoes are ruined," she cried out loudly in dismay. The man rolled his eyes while trying to calm her.

"Shouldn't be too hard to get away from her," Hannah muttered under her breath to the boys, grinning in spite of her fear at how silly the woman looked.

"What was that you said?" the woman asked sharply.

"The Cloud Juicer . . . it's this way," Hannah said to her, pointing to the far end of the island, as they marched out onto the concrete walking bridge that connected the riverbank to the island.

Once they reached the island, Elliot, Miguel and Hannah were easily able to speed ahead of their kidnappers as the woman walked carefully on her tiptoes over the soggy grass.

Hannah glanced back over her shoulder. "We could make a run for it now," she said excitedly when they were out of hearing distance.

Miguel glanced back at two adults following them. "One problem . . . that man still has a gun in his pocket," he said uneasily.

"I think Miguel is right. You're the fastest runner Hannah . . . you have to stay on the ground." Elliot said. "Miguel and I will climb the tree and try to sidetrack the guy while you make a run for help."

"But since I told them I took the Cloud Juicer, they'll be suspicious if I don't show them where it is," She replied doubtfully.

"I know," Miguel said excitedly in his movie director's voice. "Run ahead of us and fall down, pretend like you've twisted your ankle." They were almost to the clump of trees at the far end of the island so Hannah raced ahead of them. Just before she reached the trees, she tripped and rolled over, immediately grabbing at her ankle and calling out in pain.

"Oh, great," the man said as he came running up. "Are you okay?" Much to their surprise, he seemed genuinely concerned. He offered his hand to Hannah.

Hannah stood up but didn't put any weight on her left ankle. "I can't climb the tree. Elliot and Miguel can show you where it is," she said with a grimace, keeping her eyes on her supposedly injured leg.

The woman finally made it to the end of the island and she stood close to Hannah while Elliot and Miguel started to make their way up toward the hiding spot, scampering up the tree that leaned gently over the river. Miguel slipped on the wet bark of the tree and almost fell but the man reached out and steadied him. "I better come up there with you," he said. High above them, the graceful cypress boughs danced crazily in the wind.

Elliot led the way slowly up the taller, middle tree, his foot slipping several times off of the slats of wood nailed to the tree that were used for climbing. Elliot slid carefully out onto the limb just above the hiding spot. He made room for Miguel beside him but the man remained several feet below, draping one arm around the main trunk of the tree with one hand while supporting himself with one foot on a lower limb and one foot on a slat.

"Hurry up and get the Cloud . . . –" the man started to say impatiently. But a commotion below caught his attention. Hannah had been waiting for just the right moment to make her break. With the boys out on the limb and out of reach of the man, she stomped down hard on the woman's right foot and then kicked her hard in the shin. The woman yelped in pain as she raised her foot and then toppled over as she tried to stand on one leg. Hannah raced away, the strong wind sweeping her hair off of her face.

"Come back here!" Hannah heard the woman's shrill voice screaming behind her and she ran even faster. Back across the island Hannah sprinted. The river was starting to spill onto the walking bridge as she crossed and water splashed over Hannah as she ran. Just as she reached the riverbank, she spotted two police cars pull up and block the entrance to the park.

"Here we are . . . help!" Hannah screamed as she ran up the hill toward them. Her words were whipped away by the wind.

"Why did you let her get away?" The man shouted furiously at the woman below. "Take those stupid heels off and go after her." He watched the woman kick off her shoes and jog toward the walking bridge.

Elliot whispered to Miguel. "You've gotta keep him busy while I get the jumping rope for us," he said, pointing to the rope hanging over the water about midway out on the limb.

"You want us to jump into the river?" Miguel looked down at the rapidly flowing dark water below him in alarm.

"No. We're going to try something I've always wondered about doing," Elliot grinned. "Trust me."

"How am I going to distract him?" Miguel glanced over at the man who was still watching the woman chase after Hannah.

"You want to be an actor. Now is your chance," Elliot said in a low voice as he started inching out on the limb toward the rope.

They both flinched when the man turned and shouted up to them. "Get the Cloud Juicer right now or someone is going to get hurt."

Miguel slowly moved back toward the hiding spot and stuck his arm deep into the tree, intentionally scratching his hand on a sharp edge inside the hollow. Then he let out a piercing scream. "My hand . . . my hand," he screamed in pain. "A tree snake bit me." Tears flowed down his cheeks.

The man turned pale. "There are tree snakes?" He looked anxiously at Miguel and then longingly down at the ground. "Are you faking this kid? Like your little pal faked her ankle?" The man studied Miguel's bloody hand while Eliot crept back toward Miguel with the rope in his hand.

At the entrance to the park, one of the police officers turned in amazement to see a small girl wearing mud-splattered clothes running toward them. Her long, rain-soaked, brown hair was pasted to her head. He ran over and knelt down beside her. Gasping for breath, Hannah stood clutching her side that ached from running so hard with one hand and put her other hand on his shoulder for support.

"What are you doing out here alone in this storm?" he asked with concern. "Hey, aren't you Mike Dawson's girl?" He hadn't recognized her at first since she was covered with mud.

Hannah nodded but she was still too out of breath to speak.

"Your daddy's gonna pitch a fit when he finds out you're down here," the police officer said sternly. "You oughta have more sense than this."

Finally she spoke. "The bad guys are down there . . . they have Elliot and Miguel . . . they kidnapped us . . . they're trying to steal the professor's Cloud Juicer." She ran out of breath again and stopped talking.

"Whoa . . . slow down there . . . did you say a kidnapping?"

The other police officer held a pair of binoculars to his eyes. "I don't believe it. There are three people up in a tree on far end of the island," he said in dismay.

Hannah looked at the man in disbelief. "Isn't that why you're here? To find us?"

"We're here to stop anyone from going into the park. There's a twenty-foot wall of water coming down the El Toro toward Cypress Springs and it's going to hit here any minute. Anyone left down there will be swept away by the river," he said in a clipped voice.

Hannah screamed and started to run back toward the river. "Elliot . . . Miguel," she cried out as loud as she could. The tall, muscular police officer grabbed Hannah and held her close to him as she kicked and screamed, trying to get away so she could warn her friends.

"Honey, there isn't anything we can do for them now. The flood waters will reach them before we can," he said sadly.

"Noooooo . . . it's all my fault that we are here," Hannah shrieked and she began to sob. "I told them the Cloud Juicer was on the island."

Her wailing was drowned out by the ear-splitting distress signal the other police officer sounded, trying to warn the others left on the island of the approaching danger.

Chapter 16

"I'm not sticking my hand back in there," Miguel said, still sobbing over his imaginary snakebite. He pointed to the hollow in the tree. "You get the Cloud Juicer," he said to the man.

The man held up his hand. "Shut up. What's that noise . . . it sounds like a foghorn or something." He turned and looked over his shoulder to the entrance of the park and let out a string of bad words. "The cops are on to us," he shouted angrily when he spotted the two police cars. Elliot quietly slipped part of the rope into Miguel's hands.

But when the man turned back to face Miguel, what he saw terrified him even more than the police. "Ahhhhhhhhhhhhhhhhhhhh," he screamed.

Elliot and Miguel jerked their heads around to look behind them. They couldn't believe their eyes when they saw the wall of water barreling down the river toward them. In a matter of minutes they would all be swept away by the floodwaters.

"Now," screamed Elliot to Miguel in total panic. "Kick off hard and don't let go of the rope until I tell you." Miguel hesitated. "Jump!" Elliot commanded. They swung out over the river but instead of letting go when they reached the middle of the channel, the boys hung on and the momentum of their weight carried them close to the other side of the river.

"Let go NOW!" Elliot cried out. Elliot landed in shallow water at the edge of the riverbank and the rapidly moving water started to sweep him away. He struggled against the current, clawing desperately for a hold in the slimy mud of the riverbank. Miguel, who had landed on the edge of the bank, grabbed Elliot's hand and helped him out of the water.

The river was rising rapidly ahead of the floodwaters and the boys struggled to climb up the riverbank fast enough to stay above the water line. It would be a tough climb to the top; the bank on this side of the river was steep and covered with brush. Almost blinded by rain and mud, the boys scrambled up the hill on hands and knees. Brambles shredded Miguel's colorful jogging suit, exposing a cut on his leg. Elliot screamed out as a sharp branch punctured his left hand.

Near the top, Elliot and Miguel paused to look for a foothold. The top four feet of the bank were almost vertical and there was no brush for them to grab on to.

"We're not gonna make it," Miguel called out in alarm as he gasped for breath.

Elliot's heart was pounding so hard he thought it would explode. "We might be high enough," he cried out over the roar of the river that boiled past them only a couple feet below. The roots of the small brush that Elliot clung too started to give way and he slipped a few inches back down the bank. He screamed and frantically reached out to grab onto another small tree.

Then a loud voice boomed out above them. "Give me your hands." Elliot and Miguel looked up to see Hannah's father hanging upside down with a rope attached to his waist. He extended one of his large paw-like hands to each of them and Elliot and Miguel reached out to him. Then they were slowly pulled up onto the top of the riverbank where paramedics immediately wrapped the boys in blankets. For a couple of minutes, Elliot and Miguel stood shivering, while rescue workers bustled around them.

Elliot glanced down and realized he was still wearing the yellow ribbon he had won at Field Day only a couple hours earlier on a string around his neck. The ribbon was muddy and a couple drops of blood covered some of the words. After being kidnapped and nearly drowning in the river, winning the long jump competition didn't seem very important to Elliot anymore.

Then the sound of a helicopter nearby drew Elliot and Miguel back to the edge of the riverbank and they watched it fly toward the brown-haired man who was clinging to the highest limb of their secret hiding place tree. The island had completely disappeared under the now raging El Toro River. A rope ladder dropped from the helicopter and the man grabbed for it urgently, pulling himself up into the helicopter.

Not only was the island covered with water but most of the city park on the other side of the river was submerged as well. Elliot and Miguel could see that the river was even starting to splash over the top of the Grand Avenue Bridge.

"Look, there's Hannah!" Elliot cried out excitedly. He and Miguel waved franticly at her as she stood near the police cars still parked at the entrance to the park on the other side of the river. She was jumping up and down and waving her arms back at them. They watched as one of the police officers forced the red-haired lady into the back seat of one of the police cars.

"Wow . . . look at that," Miguel yelled. He pointed to the car they had been driven to the park in, now crumbled like a piece of paper against one of the concrete footings of the Grand Avenue Bridge.

Elliot and Miguel heard someone clear his throat beside them and they looked up. "Maybe not such a good day to be playing by the river boys," Hannah's father said solemnly in his deep voice. For the first time of what would be many more times that afternoon, the boys told their story of being kidnapped and taken to the island by burglars who wanted to steal Professor Brown's Cloud Juicer.

"Hannah's okay . . . see, she' over there!" Miguel pointed across the river.

"I know. Lucky for you she's safe or I'd throw you back in the river," Mr. Dawson said with his booming laugh. Miguel and Elliot were pretty sure he was only joking.

About an hour later, Elliot's father walked into the back door of his house and into the kitchen. "Honey, I'm home," he called out, dropping his luggage to the floor. "Can you believe that storm today?" Crocket rushed into the kitchen to greet him.

Jon Brown sorted through the mail he picked up from the counter and then he wandered into the living room where he thought he heard voices. "Anything exciting happen while I was gone?"

When he looked up from a letter he was reading, his puzzled eyes swept across the faces of his wife and his father to Miguel's and Hannah's parents. Then his chin dropped when he noticed a female uniformed police officer standing beside them and the books and tapes scattered around the room. Finally his astonished gaze rested on Elliot, Hannah and Miguel who sat silently on the sofa wrapped in over-sized towels looking like three waterlogged enchiladas.

"Someone please tell me what's going on," he stammered, as he dropped into a chair. Everyone started to talk at once. Crocket wagged his tale in excitement; two parties in one day. He was in dog heaven.

Chapter 17

"Oh, man . . . I'm finally a celebrity and I look awful," Miguel groaned in dismay, pointing to the picture on the front page of the *Cypress Springs Express News* the next morning. Elliot and Hannah crowded around him to look at the newspaper Miguel had spread out on the front porch of the Brown house. The picture featured all three of them under the headline: Local Youth Foil Kidnapping Attempt. Their hair was plastered to their heads and their clothes were muddy. Miguel's right cheek was puffy and scraped.

"Nothing wrong with the picture. That's the way you always look." Hannah winked at Elliot. Elliot grinned.

"You don't look any worse than we do," Elliot said, studying the picture of their dirty, unsmiling faces. "I think we look like the bad guys." He closed his eyes and lay back in the warm, bright sunshine flooding the porch. For the first time this week the deep blue sky was clear of clouds. Then images of yesterday's storm and their narrow escape from the flooding El Toro River crowded Elliot's mind and he sat up with a shiver.

"I don't want to go the river for a week," he exclaimed. Just then he spotted his grandfather get out of his car and walk toward them. "Grandpa's back from the police station." Elliot and his friends pounced on Professor Brown, demanding to know more about their kidnappers.

"Are they spies?" Elliot tugged on his grandfather's arm.

"Are they double agents?" Hannah asked in a hushed voice.

"Were they going to use the Cloud Juicer to take over the world?" Miguel waved his arms wildly.

Professor Brown laughed so hard his big tummy jiggled up and down as he gathered all three of them into his arms for a hug. "What are we going to do with you three?"

He released them and they continued on and sat on the steps of the front porch. "Turns out this man and woman are just small time thieves who wanted to steal my Cloud Juicer design. They thought they were going to become millionaires selling the Cloud Juicer on cable television for three easy payments of $19.95," he said with a chuckle.

"Would they have gotten rich?" Miguel asked in an awe-struck voice.

"Who knows? People will buy just about anything they see advertised on television," Professor Brown said in amusement.

"You could get rich," Elliot said excitedly, imagining stacks of money all around them.

"Maybe. But there's one small problem. I hadn't finished work on the Cloud Juicer and it's still missing. Your kidnappers insist they don't have it," he said sadly.

He went on, "It's too bad though. I was having fun working on it and who knows maybe someday I could have made super Cloud Juice."

Hannah cleared her throat and kicked at the grass with her toe. "Professor Brown, sir, I took your Cloud Juicer and hid it," she said softly.

"Oh right, Hannah. That was a great story yesterday but I don't think it'll work again today," Elliot said with a laugh, poking Hannah's shoulder. They all stared at Hannah who remained silent and realized she wasn't joking.

"I was afraid Elliot and maybe even Miguel would actually drink the Cloud Juice and get hurt by it so I took it out of your workshop and hid it under your back porch," Hannah said.

"Elliot and I had a conversation about that at Field Day yesterday and I think he understands now that he doesn't need anything, including Cloud Juice, to be a winner." Professor Brown's stern look made Elliot's cheeks turn slightly pink.

They all followed Hannah to her hiding spot and watched her scoot under the porch. In less than a minute she crawled back out holding the Cloud Juicer and gave it to Professor Brown. Overjoyed to have his invention back in hand, the professor headed toward his workshop, humming absentmindedly as he walked away.

"I'm so tired of hearing about Cloud Juice," Miguel said, covering his ears with his hands as they all flopped down on Elliot's front porch again.

"What are we going to do for fun this summer? Hannah asked, her eyes lighting up with excitement. "School will be out in only two more weeks."

"I'm not taking that dumb craft class again this summer," Miguel said hotly.

"It wasn't dumb. It was artistic just like the movies you make," Hannah replied.

"No way," Miguel howled with laughter. "It's not even close to movies."

Elliot barely listened to them argue back and forth. He sat very still watching a squirrel carefully run along a utility wire crossing the street.

"Ah ha!" shouted Elliot. "I know what we can do this summer."

Miguel and Hannah stopped bickering and stared at him in alarm. They'd seen that faraway look in Elliot's eyes before – just before the three of them got into trouble. Big trouble.